Content Warning: This book contains rape/sexual assault, abuse, graphic sex scenes, homosexuality, police brutality, and homicide.

Tales From the Darkside: I Prey, You Kill for Me

By

C. K. TARVER

Published by: Tina J Presents

ISBN: 9798864597613

Chapter 1: Sierra "Sting" Matthews

I stood in the shadows of the darkness and waited for Marvin to come out of the well-lit two-family flat. For the last few days, I listened as he harassed Aaron by telling him he wasn't shit and would never be shit. When he got drunk, the verbal abuse turned physical, and Aaron's cries could be heard in the middle of the night. I waited for him to speak those magic words and I would be happy to grant his wishes.

Aaron was my thirteen-year-old neighbor, whose family lived across the street from me in our middle-class neighborhood. His mother worked long hours, so he spent a lot of time with his stepfather, Marvin.

Marvin was a mean-spirited man who drank way more than he should have. Unfortunately, he took his anger out on Aaron and his mother, Angela. Sometimes I think Angela worked long hours because she didn't want to deal with Marvin's alcoholic ass. If Aaron wasn't involved, I wouldn't give two fucks, but sparing her own life so her son can suffer was unacceptable. The only reason why she didn't feel my wrath was because the foster system in Michigan sucked. I hoped Marvin's upcoming demise would allow Angela time to focus on herself and treat Aaron the way he should be treated. If not, she too would have to disappear as well, fuck it. Mistreating kids was unacceptable. Even though it wasn't my business, Marvin made it my business the moment I overheard him abuse Aaron.

I wanted to intervene when I heard Aaron cry for help, but fear of being exposed halted my decision. I knew it would cause more harm than good, so I waited.

The constant abuse was becoming too much for me to bear. I gave up hope that his mother would ever wake up and leave Marvin. Aaron turned to the only person he thought could hear his cry, or so he thought. After Aaron finished sobbing, he prayed to God that Marvin be removed from him and his mother's life. Thanks to his prayer, Marvin was one full moon away from never being able to hurt another child again. And I was honored to be the person to make it happen.

I kept my distance as I followed Marvin as he staggered towards the liquor store. He left a lingering smell of alcohol that invaded my space as I pursued him. The moon was coming to full circle, and I felt the burning sensation of my whiskers protruding out of my face like an adolescent going through puberty. When I felt the full transition start to take place, I ducked into the nearby alley. It had only been a short time since I became a werewolf, so I was still getting used to the pain of the mutation.

I tore the clothes off my body because they created a burning sensation that was painful and unbearable. My bones cracked and transformed from my human form into the skeletal resemblance of a wolf, and my canine teeth and sharp nails ripped through my skin.

By the time the transformation was complete, Marvin had made it to the store and was walking out with a bottle of Paul Masson, wrapped in a brown paper bag. I watched from the alley as he got halfway down the block, opened the bottle, and placed it up to his lips. Even from the alley I could smell the alcohol, mixed with funky ass breath. Marvin stood in one spot and drank most of the contents in the bottle, before he staggered to his demise. Moments before he approached the alley, I jumped out, blocking his view. He rubbed his eyes to make sure what he was seeing was real, before taking another sip.

"Either you're a big fucking dog or the rumor that wolves in this neighborhood is true," he laughed as he tried to stagger around me.

"I can't allow you to hurt him anymore," I roared.

"And you talk, too? Unfucking believable!" He laughed.

I stared at Marvin, as he laughed hysterically like I was a fucking joke.

"Okay, for kicks, who is it you can't allow me to hurt anymore?" he inquired.

"Aaron."

"Aaron? That little bastard of a child by that bitch, Angela? Fuck him and fuck her," he spat.

Slash!

I went across Marvin's chest with my left paw, leaving his dingy shirt bloody and shredded. The brown paper bag crashed to the ground.

"Son of a bitch! You made me drop my liquor! That's your motherfucking ass, you hairy piece of shit!" Marvin said, not giving a fuck about being slashed. He was only concerned with his drink.

Marvin stood in a boxer stance, and danced around me as he threw wild jabs in the air. I tried to be serious and kill the motherfucker off, but this shit was hilarious! Never in my history of eating or killing a motherfucker have they ever tried to box me. Usually, I had screamers, and runners, but never a boxer.

This motherfucker was drunk as fuck!

The smell of the alcohol spewed from his pores, mouth, and nose, and I caught the smell of all that shit.

I lured Marvin into the alley by backing up and pretending to be scared. Like a dumb ass he followed and started to taunt me.

"Uh huh, your lil furry ass can't fuck with this. Back in day I stung like a butterfly and floated like a bee!" he said totally fucking up the late great Muhammad Ali's famous quote.

"Why the fuck you care so much about Aaron? That lil nigga ain't going to be shit. He's going to be just as worthless as his mother," Marvin yelled.

"Worthless men like you are the reason why females switch to the other side?" I stated as I inched closer to him.

"Oh, you're a bitch huh? I ain't never had no werewolf pussy before, but it's a first time for everything." Marvin said as he stopped fighting the air, unzipped his pants and let his dick fall out.

Marvin was working with a monster! I see why Angela stayed with his ass. Not only was he beating her ass, but he was also putting a hurting on her pussy too!

"Yeah, bitch. You like that huh?" he asked as he stroked himself.

"Come howl on this dick." He said with a laugh.

No longer interested in playing games with his big dick ass, I opened my mouth, bent down, and bit his dick off, taking several of his fingers with it. Marvin fell to his knees and screamed to the top of his lungs. I removed his dick from my mouth and stuffed it down his throat to muffle his cries.

I started beating the shit out of him like I imagined he'd beaten Aaron and his mom. The sound of Marvin's bone breaking underneath my feet and fist gave me great satisfaction.

Marvin laid motionless on the ground as I hovered over him.

"You're not so tough now, are you?"

Spit flew from my mouth as I taunted Marvin while he laid in a pool of blood, urine, and feces.

"Fuck you bitch!" he managed to say after he spit his dick out his mouth and into my face.

I licked my face with my tongue and let out a sinister laugh.

"No fuck you." I countered as I opened my mouth as wide as I could and bit down on Marvin's neck and chewed until his vein busted, and blood exploded inside of my mouth. Although Marvin was no longer moving, I didn't stop until his head was completely severed from his body. Afterwards, I moved to his battered chest and stomach, and ripped out his insides. One by one I snatched out his intestines (small and large), his liver, kidney and, finally his heart.

Lights from the apartments above caught my attention. I took a final look at what was left of Marvin and walked down the alley in the opposite direction from which I entered. I retreated to the only safe place I knew where to go to transition back, the woods. Once I found my special spot, that only I was aware of, I laid down and licked myself free of Marvin's blood. Afterwards, I closed my eyes, fell asleep and waited until I turned back into the human form of myself. I smiled as I imagined a happy

Aaron enjoying life once again. I also thought about my pre-werewolf days and what turned me into the beast I was today. I never set out to hurt anybody, but I couldn't let them get away with what they did to me. Every one of them had to pay.

*****

When I was younger, I was interested in joining a crew who called themselves The Seven Mile Wolf Pack. They represented red and walked the southwest streets of Detroit like they ruled them. The crew was mixed with Latino, Black, Hispanic, and a few kids that were white-Hispanics. Seven Mile Wolf Pack was the melting pot for everyone, no matter your race. I remembered when I approached the crew about joining. It was a day I could never forget, no matter how hard I tried.

I sat on the porch of our rundown four family flat and watched as the crew strutted down the street. When they walked past my house, I jumped off the porch and blocked their path.

"I would like to join y'all pack," I said boldly.

"Is that right? What makes you think you would be a good fit for our pack?" said one of the guys I assumed was the leader.

"Because I'm about that fucking life and can fuck a bitch up," I responded.

"We all can fuck a bitch up, what makes you so special?" One of the smart mouth females commented.

"Do you want to be the first one to find out?" I threatened as I stepped in her face.

"Puta, I will kick your fuckin ass!" She resorted back and pushed me.

I retaliated by punching her in her eye and throwing blow after blow, connecting with her face, head, and body hoping she would fall so I could stomp the shit out of her. Unfortunately, I underestimated her, because she came back on some Floyd Mayweather shit! That bitch hit me with a combination so out cold I thought I was in a McDonald's drive thru!

Not to be outdone, I did what a lot of motherfuckers do when they start to lose the fight, I rushed the bitch. When she fell to the ground, I jumped on top of her and started to fuck her up, but she was not giving up. She flipped me over and beat the shit out of me until one of the guys pulled her off me.

"Okay that's enough Kris. I think she got the picture," he laughed, with a little twang in his voice, I could tell he had a little sugar in his tank.

I stood up, brushed my clothes off, and wiped the blood from my mouth.

"What's your name?" said the guy who pulled the girl off me.

"Sierra," I answered.

"I think I'm going to call you Sting, because you were going round for round with Kris ass!" He laughed as he mocked me by throwing his fist in the air.

Kris looked at me like she wanted to go another round, but even she had to acknowledge my hand game.

"You got some squabble, Chica, but don't ever try that shit again. Dash isn't going to save your ass next time," Kris warned.

"Anytime, Chica," I challenged her.

"Enough!" The leader, whose name was Blaze yelled.

The guy next to him whispered in his ear, causing him to smirk.

"Kris, Dash and Sherrie, walk!" he demanded, and the ladies walked ahead, with Dash following behind them. When Kris walked past me, she rolled her eyes at me so hard, I thought they were going to get stuck. I was left with

the leader and four members of the crew. They were eyeing me up and down.

"My name is Blaze, and this is Kold, Slime, Thor, and Duke. Are you serious about joining this pack?" he asked.

"Fuck yeah," I answered.

"Meet us at the vacant warehouse on 5th and Victor at eight o'clock," Thor demanded.

"For what?" I inquired.

"Do you want to be in the pack or not?" Kold asked.

"Yeah," I responded.

"We will see you at eight, and come alone," Blaze said as he turned and walked away.

I looked at the men as they walked down the street. A chill ran through my body. My gut was telling me not to go, but the feeling of wanting a family made me stay.

I arrived at the warehouse at eight o'clock sharp. It was empty, cold, and damp. The only light that was visible was from a streetlight on the corner of the block. I made sure my knife was secure in my bra, it was one of my prize possessions that was given to me by my father. He said the knife was special because the blade was made with silver, in case I ever encountered a werewolf. The irony of that!

My daddy believed in all that shit. Witches, ghosts, vampires, werewolves, you name it. We had so much sage, silver, and crosses in our house, you would think he was crazy.

Footsteps behind me took me out of my trance. I turned around to see the crew from earlier, minus the ladies and Dash.

"What's up? What do I have to do?" I asked, preparing to get jumped in. My face and body were already coated with Vaseline.

"Take that shit off," Blaze instructed as he looked at my body and smiled.

"What?" I asked, thinking I heard him wrong.

He stepped closer to me. I thought my eyes were playing tricks on me.

Did his eyes just shift?

I stared at him but didn't move.

Blaze ripped open my blouse and looked hungrily at my breast. When I turned around to run, he grabbed me, tackled me to the ground and started to tear the rest of my clothes off. The other men joined in to help as I screamed, kicked and begged for them to stop.

"Put something in her mouth to shut her up," Blaze demanded.

"Helppppp!!" I yelled, hoping somebody heard my cries.

Slime tore my shirt, balled it up, and stuffed it in my mouth. He took the other piece of the torn shirt and bonded my hands together as tears fell down my cheeks. My panties

were ripped off my ass and my legs were parted.

"You will forever be mine; I'm marking my

territory." Blaze whispered in my ear, before he forcefully

entered me.

I tried to scream, because the pain was

excruciating. I wasn't no virgin or nothing, so outside of

my pussy being completely dry, I wasn't sure why it hurt so

much. He had to be about fourteen inches long.

Blaze pumped me as the others removed their

clothes and readied themselves for their turn. I etched each

one of their faces in my head because I was going to make

their asses pay, if I made it out alive.

When Blaze climaxed and came inside of me, he

started to howl, and the others followed suit. As soon as he

pulled out, Kold entered me, but I couldn't really feel

anything because Blaze had already stretched me out. He

removed his dick from my pussy and forced it inside of my ass.

I tried to scream, but my shirt stuffed inside of my mouth muffled my efforts as Kold violated my virgin ass. He slapped my ass and laughed as he fucked me repeatedly. When he got ready to cum, he pulled out and came all over my back. The other men followed suit and had their way with me as well.

After Duke finished, Blaze stood up and stroked himself. He had a massive dick and big ass muscles I didn't notice earlier. I looked him dead in his eyes and his eyes shifted again, the same as earlier. I took another look at his dick, and it looked like it grew two more inches right before my eyes! When he positioned himself between my legs again, I passed out.

Soon after, I was awakened by a frantic Dash. That was the day my life changed forever.

Two months later, I found out I was pregnant with Blaze's baby. I immediately told Dash and he googled the location of the abortion clinic he'd accompanied Tonya, his sister, to several times before. Dash stayed by my side every step of the way and we became the best of friends.

Unfortunately, Blaze was correct when he said I will always be his territory. The night he raped me, our bodily fluids intertwined, and I became a hybrid werewolf. I learned two things from this experience; that my father was right, werewolves do exist and two, I was going to make Blaze and his crew pay for what they had done to me.

Chapter 2: Caesar Jacobs

My name is Caesar Jacobs. I was born on the rough streets of Detroit in a rundown eastside apartment. When I was nine months old, my white father decided he didn't want to be a father anymore, so he left my mother and me to fend for ourselves. Two months later, we were homeless and on the streets.

Coming from a one parent household, my mother struggled to make ends meet. By the time I was school age, she had two more kids and we bounced from pillar to post. There were plenty of times my siblings and I went without food, clothing, or shelter. But my mother was our true hero, she sacrificed everything for us, and I will always owe her my life for it.

My mother convinced my maternal grandmother to allow me to move in with her until she got herself together.

At six years of age, I was separated from my mother and my siblings, and I had a hard time adjusting to life outside of the hood.

From the first day I started elementary school, life was hell. My brown curly hair, light skin and green eyes were confusing to both the black and white kids. There were times I questioned who and what I was, which made me depressed. I dreaded going to school because I was constantly being bullied. As a result, when I was home, I stayed in my bedroom and barely interacted with my family. After my fifth-grade graduation, my grandmother packed up my things and sent me back to live with my mother.

Unlike other people, I became a werewolf on my own accord. I never felt I belonged, so becoming a part of a secret society was welcoming. I remember when I first stumbled upon the Howling Huskies.

A full moon was approaching when I saw a group of people walking towards the woods located at the end of the cul-de-sac. I jumped off the porch and decided to follow them. For years, it was rumored wolves congregated in the woods whenever there was a full moon. Today I was going to find out.

By the time I caught up to them, they had all gathered in the center of the woods and were surrounded by tree stumps and logs. One of the members of the pack started a fire with an array of sticks they gathered. I stood behind a tree and watched as the pack of friends removed their clothes and stood in front of each other, naked as the day they came out of their mother's womb.

One of the males started howling. I assumed he was the Alpha because he was very masculine and had a certain aura about himself. Everyone followed suit and started howling as they stared at the moon.

This explained the noises I mistook for dogs I was hearing in the middle of the night.

The clouds dancing around the moon dissipated and a full moon was born. I paid extra attention to the only woman of the pack. She was gorgeous. The glow from the moonlight made her look like a goddess. I was so mesmerized by her beauty that I stumbled over a branch and fell, causing everyone to look in my direction.

I tried to gain my composure before they gained up on me.

"I'm sorry to interrupt, but I want to be down with your crew!" I stated.

The sexy female growled and caught me off guard.

"Whoa, chill baby girl, I don't mean no harm!" I said smoothly.

"Why are you here?" The Alpha male asked.

"I heard a lot of good things about y'all, and I think I will be a perfect fit. All my life, I've never felt like I belonged. I think I found that in this crew," I informed him.

"You don't know anything about us, or what you're getting into," he scorned me.

"It doesn't matter. It can't be any worse than the hell I'm going through right now. Nobody gives a fuck about me. I think this is where I belong," I begged.

"You "think" this is where you belong? This is not a decision you need to think about. Once you cross over, the only way you're crossing back over is death," the Alpha barked.

"I have nothing to lose," I said as the female from earlier inched closer to me, exposing her canine teeth.

"Are you sure about this?" one of the other members asked.

"Absolutely," I responded as the chic pounced on me and tackled me to the ground.

I tried to fight her, but she was extremely strong. I looked in her fiery red eyes and felt an instant connection when she relaxed and calmed down a bit. She was so close, I thought she was going to kiss me. Like a fool, I closed my eyes, and puckered my lips to welcome her. The feeling of fur on my face and hot breath made me open my eyes, but it was too late. She bit the side of my neck causing me to scream out in pain.

"Arrrgghh!"

I tried to wrestle her off, but I was no match for her massive strength. She growled as she bit deeper. The pain was so horrific I was unable to scream or fight. I laid numb, and in a state of shock.

By the time she released me, I immediately felt different. I could hear the horn of the train ten miles away; the cries of a baby at a nearby apartment, and the delightful smell of blood from steaks being cooked at a local steakhouse.

Suddenly, I felt thirsty, and my head was pounding. When I grabbed my head, I noticed hair sprouting from my wrist. I opened my mouth to scream, only to start howling, causing everyone to howl too. My body felt like it was burning from the inside out, so I ripped my clothes off and let them fall to my feet. My bones protruded from my skin and my body was covered with fur.

Everyone began going through their own transition. The chic that bit me had completely turned, as well as the Alpha male. One by one, the others transformed into werewolves. We spent the rest of the night howling in the woods until the early hours of the morning.

When I woke up, I was cold, naked, shivering and alone. I looked around in search of my clothes, but only saw shredded rags laying on the mist-covered ground.

"Damn, I can't walk through the hood with my dick swinging," I whispered.

"No, you can't," she said.

I turned around and saw the chic that bit me standing there with clothes in her hand. I covered my dick.

"I already saw it, nice package," she complimented as she held out the clothes.

"Thanks," I responded as I grabbed the clothes, and put them on.

"Nobody said it would be so painful, and you could've given a brother a heads up before you bit the shit out of me," I informed her as I rubbed my neck and stretched.

"You were talking too much. Besides, it's always less painful when you don't anticipate it," she advised.

"Hell, I can't tell, where are the others?" I asked.

"Home, work, I don't know," she shrugged.

"What's next?" I asked out of curiosity.

I had only been a werewolf for a few short hours, and I wanted to know more.

"Give it a few days, it takes some getting used to," she informed me with a smile.

"Get use to what?" I questioned.

"You will see," she smiled and turned to walk away.

"I didn't get your name," I called out.

"Chili. My name is Chili,"

"My name is Caesar."

"I know your name,"

"When can I see you again?" I asked.

"Duh, the next full moon,"

I watched as Chili left the woods.

Unfortunately, shortly after my initiation, the leader, and several other members of the pack, including Chili, were gunned down by a team of hunters that had been watching them from afar. Several omega wolves were able to escape with our lives, but the pack no longer had a leader and none of the omega wolves were willing to step up, so they nominated me, and I accepted. For the first time in my life, I felt like I belonged, and I was going to do everything in my power to protect my newfound family.

Chapter 3: Dillan "Dash" Chavers

My situation was like both Caesar and Sting. I never felt like I belonged or was accepted, so I looked for love in the streets because I had no other choice. I was a "PK", a preacher's kid raised in a two-parent household. At a young age, I flaunted around the house in my mother and sister's clothes and shoes. They thought it was cute that I liked to play dress up. When I got older, and graduated to makeup, shit hit the fan.

When I was eleven years old, my mother and father came home early from a church function. My older sister Tonya and I were playing with my mother's makeup and clothes when my mother busted in the room. She almost had a heart attack when she saw me in full drag with a "beat" face. She put her hands over her mouth and gasped. My dumb ass thought she was speechless at how good I looked, so I paraded around the room and modeled for her. It was all fun and games until my father walked in.

The look on my father's face told me I had fucked up. He almost broke his neck, trying to get a piece of me. My mother stepped in front of him to prevent my father from attacking me, but he pushed her onto the floor like a rag doll and charged at me like a raging pit bull. Seconds later, his hands were wrapped around my neck, and I was fighting for my life.

Tonya screamed at my father as she bounced on his back and beat him with her small fist. Unphased by my sister's blows, my father scolded me while he choked the life out of me.

"No son of mind is going to be no sissy!" My father yelled with tears in his eyes.

"I will kill your ass before I allow your homosexual ways to spill into this family!" he continued.

I saw the hurt in my father's face as I struggled to breathe. Everything was starting to go dark, and Tonya's and my father's screams were becoming unrecognizable.

Boom!

"Get the fuck off of my son!" I heard my mother say as she fired the gun, then pointed the shot gun at my father's head.

"Carole, what in God's name are you doing?" My father asked my mother in disbelief as he dropped me on the floor and walked towards her. We were all shocked because my mother had never raised her voice at my father, let alone curse him. The sound of the gun being cocked again stopped my father dead in his tracks. My mother pointed the gun at my father's head again.

"Dillan Michael Chavers Sr. if you ever put your hands around our son's neck again, I will send you to motherfucking glory," my mother yelled.

My father stood frozen and stunned at my mother's behavior. Tonya helped me off the floor, and we cautiously maneuvered our way around my father as he pleaded with my mother.

"Carole, the boy is around here parading in women's clothes with a face full of makeup that looks better than yours, what the hell am I supposed to do?" My father cried.

"Talk to him, Dillan, not kill him," my mother instructed him.

"What the hell am I supposed to say to him?" my father questioned.

"I don't know. You call on the Lord for everything else, ask him to guide your steps. But if you ever pull this shit again, I'm going to send you to your Lord, and y'all can have the conversation, personally. Do I make myself clear?" my mother warned.

My father nodded in defeat, as he flopped on the bed and covered his face with his hands in disgust. My mother ushered us out of the room and closed the bedroom door behind her. I could still hear my father's cries as my mother and sister escorted me down the hall to the bathroom in silence. When we were safe in the bathroom, and I felt my father was no longer a threat, I spoke.

"Ma, can I ask you something?" I whispered.

"Yes Dillan," she responded calmly.

"Do you think my makeup is better than yours, like daddy said?" I asked sincerely.

My mother tried to muffle her laugh with her hand.

"Chile, you are beat to the Gods!" My mother whispered as she continued laughing, causing Tonya and I to laugh as well.

My mother pulled Tonya and I in for a tight hug. I could tell she was crying, but I wasn't sure why. Maybe she knew something I didn't know. Maybe she came to the realization that she had lost her only son and gained

another daughter.

We never spoke on the day my father choked me out again. Instead, my father made sure I breathe, ate, and shit at the church. I guess he figured he can pray the gay out of me. Little did he know, his church was filled with young boys and men like me, and it was the breeding ground for homosexuality. It was also the first place I had my first sexual encounter with another male, but that's a story for another day.

*****

I asked to join the Seven Mile Wolf Pack after my father grew tired of my flamboyant ways and kicked me out. Although my mother didn't agree with my lifestyle, she accepted me for who I was. My father, on the other hand, wasn't so accepting. One day he barged into my room while I was getting ready for school. He freaked out when he saw a sequin bra and booty shorts on my bed that I had planned on giving to Kris to hold until the party, Friday night.

My father decided he couldn't take it anymore and kicked me and my booty shorts out on the curb a week before my eighteenth birthday. Thank God, Kris's mother felt sorry for me. She let me sleep on her basement couch until I worked things out with my father. What Kris' mother didn't know was I had no intention of working shit out with my father, and her basement couch was my permanent residence.

Kris was already a member of the Seven Mile Wolf Pack. She asked Blaze, the leader, to allow me to join. He was against a gay member joining his crew, until Kris convinced him that he would be starting a new trend, and the crew would gain the support from anyone who identified with the LGBTQIA+ community. Part of my initiation was to have sex with a female. When it was first brought to my attention, I thought it was a joke, but Blaze was dead serious.

Blaze got a nearby hotel and paid a twenty-one-year-old woman one hundred dollars to bust my cherry. To my surprise, my soldier stood up as the woman, whose name I never knew grinded on me as Blaze sat in the corner and watched. When I glanced over in Blaze's direction, I could have sworn I saw him rub himself through his pants. I didn't know if he was turned on by the act, the woman's antics, or by me.

After I climaxed in the woman's mouth, he instructed me to leave. I hurriedly got dressed, walked out, and stood outside of the hotel door for a second. Moments later, I heard ass smacking and the woman screaming as if Blaze was fucking the shit out of her. As I got closer to Kris's house, I heard a howling sound. I surveyed the area before I continued up the street.

The pack did typical 'crew shit'. We terrorized other crews, sold drugs, made money, and had wild parties. We also helped clean the neighborhood, walked old ladies across the street and looked out for the younger generation. I enjoyed the family aspect of the crew, but there were some things I didn't agree with, like what Blaze and some of the crew did to a young chic name Sting, who was interested in joining the pack.

After Kris and Sting had an altercation, I figured Kris would be salty after Blaze told us to get lost as he, Kold, Duke, Slime, and Thor decided what would be the initiation process for Sting. I walked ahead, but the look in Blaze's eyes told me they were up to no good. Most of the crew were careful not to spend much one-on-one time with me because they didn't want to be mistaken for gay, so I understood why I wasn't involved in many of the processes.

I sat on Kris porched and halfway listened to her lie to Sherry and me about the ass whooping she put on Sting. Clearly, she must have forgotten we were at the same fight she was at. If anything, I would say the fight was a tie, but in no form or fashion did Kris whoop her ass. That's why I gave her the nickname of Sting, because she got them hands and didn't mind using them.

I watched as Blaze walked out of his apartment building with Thor, Duke, Slime, and Kold following close behind him. Kris noticed him as well and waved him off.

"Fuck that nigga," she huffed.

"You're only saying fuck Blaze because you're mad, he waved you off to talk to Sting," Sherry laughed.

"I ain't worried about that bitch. She's the one that needs to be worried." Kris smirked.

"What is that supposed to mean?" I asked.

"I bet any amount of money; she's getting initiated tonight." Kris said.

41

"And?" I asked.

Sherry stood up.

"I-I don't feel so good. I think I'm about to call it a night," Sherry hurried off the porch and left without another word.

"What the hell was that all about?" I asked Kris, referring to Sherry's sudden disappearance.

Kris shrugged her shoulders. I could tell it was something she wasn't telling me. I watched as Blaze and the guys hit the corner. I had a gut feeling something wasn't right.

Trusting my first instinct, I hopped off the porch and informed Kris I would be back in a minute. She said okay and disappeared into the house.

As I neared the corner, a red BMW sped up on me, almost running me over.

"What the fuck?" I cussed as I jumped up on the curb.

"Hey, lil bro!" my sister Tonya laughed.

"Tonya? You almost fuckin hit me! And whose beamer are you driving?" I questioned.

"One of my niggas bought me a car. You want to go for a ride?" Tonya asked.

"Can I get a raincheck, sis? I'm in the middle of something." I advised her as I looked around for Blaze and the others. They were nowhere in sight.

"Okay, hit me up later. I want to go shake my ass tonight." Tonya said, dancing in her seat.

"Yeah alright Ms. Thing, bye!" I yelled to her as I walked down the street, I saw the pack turn onto before Tonya's crazy ass almost ran me over.

Because it was still summer, it was still light outside. The sun had gone down, and the moon was peeking behind the clouds. There were a few kids running back and forth, screaming at one another. I looked at the kids and reminisced about the times when I was a kid.

While other boys played video games and basketball, I played house and hopscotch with the little girls.

I walked the neighborhood until the streetlights started to come on. I was about to give up and go back home, when I spotted an abandoned building on the opposite side of the tracks.

Naw, they're not in there.

I turned around and started to head back home, but a nagging feeling told me to go look inside the building. Going with my instinct, I headed towards the building.

An eerie feeling came over me and I felt something was wrong when I saw four shadows exit the building. They gave each other a dap as they disappeared in opposite directions. I picked up the pace and jogged towards the building, picking up a big stick along the way. Although I just saw who I assumed was Blaze and the pack leave, I had no idea what or who was still inside the building. I secretly prayed it wasn't Sting.

The only light in the building was the glare from the streetlights that shined through the broken windows. I turned on the flashlight of my phone and entered.

The smell of weed, crack, garbage, and other shit invaded my nostrils. I held my breath and walked from room to room looking for any signs of Sting.

"Sting!" I called out her name.

I wanted to bring awareness to her as well as to anybody that was lurking that I was on the premises.

The further I walked into a large empty space, I noticed someone lying on the ground, curled up in a fetal position. Still unaware it was Sting, I approached them with caution. When I was closer enough to realize it was Sting, I called out her name, and ran to her aid.

"Sting!" I cried out as I fell to her side.

The smell of sex and feces filled the air. I didn't know how hurt she was, or if she was even alive until she let out a moan.

"Sting! Wake up! It's me, Dash?" I yelled out of concern.

Sting tried to jump up, but she stumbled. When she pulled out a shiny knife, I gave her some room.

"Get away from me!" she cried.

The look in Sting eyes told me she was in a confused state and had no idea who I was.

"Sting, it's me, Dash. I'm here to help you. What happened to you? Did Blaze and the guys do something to you?" I questioned.

I was almost sure of what had happened but needed to be certain.

Sting collapsed to the ground and cried. Confused as to if I should comfort her or not, I just watched her until she finished crying.

"Let's get you to the hospital," I advised her as I tried to coach her to the entrance of the building.

"No! Nobody could know," she demanded.

"I don't understand. They raped you! We need to get the police involved." I yelled.

"Hell no! If I go to the police, I will be labeled as a snitch."

"Who gives a fuck, Sting! You can't allow them motherfuckers to get away with what they did. I don't know about you, but I refuse to be affiliated with known rapists. As of today, I am no longer a member of this bum ass crew! Us ladies got to stick together." I protested.

"You're right, I'm not going to let them get away with it." Sting said as she stared past me.

"So, what are you going to do?" I questioned.

"We're going to stay in the crew," Sting stated.

"Bitch, are you out of your fucking mind?" I asked in disbelief.

"Yes, the fuck I am," Sting said with a menacing grin.

"You're talking crazy right now. Let's get you home and we can talk about this later." I advised Sting as I helped her to her feet.

That was a year ago. Now we are both members of the Howling Huskies, run by that fine ass Caesar Jacobs. I had to convince Sting to join the pack. She wasn't so trusting after what Blaze and the pack did to her. But she was so smitten with Caesar, she would have done anything to be near him. And I guess the feeling was mutual, because the two of them were inseparable.

Chapter 4: Detective Sasha Grant

The sound of my cell phone ringing startled the hell out of me. I rolled over and looked at the time, it was three thirty in the morning. I   sighed deeply and reached for the phone. There was no need to complain, because this was what I signed up for. I had been trying to be a detective in the Genesee County District at the Flint Police Department for five years. There were only a few detective spots in our department and my personal relationship wasn't the best with our captain, due to the little fling we had when I first started working in the department.

When I first decided to be a police officer, I was in a bad place. My personal life was in shambles, and I needed a break. I moved out of the city of Detroit and started a new life in Flint. Moving to a place where nobody knew who I was, and vice versa gave me a clean slate, or so I thought. Sooner than later, I resorted back to my old ways and drowned myself in the one thing that kept me in trouble, but also kept me sane, sex. Although I didn't like labels, I would be what some may call a pansexual. I loved men, women, trans, whoever. If I found a person attractive, they could get it.

When my supervisor informed me, a position became available on the east side of Detroit, I was ecstatic, but apprehensive at the same time. Years ago, I left the city behind with no plans on returning. I was forced to decide between my career, and eventually coming face to face with my past, or to stay in Flint and remain stagnant? I chose my career; despite the turmoil I knew was soon to follow.

By the time I reached for the phone, it had stopped ringing. It was a missed call from my lieutenant, Jordan Masters. I gave her a call back.

"Good morning. Jordan," I answered halfway sleep.

"Detective Grant, please address me as Lt. Masters. This is not a social call," Jordan demanded.

I rolled my eyes as though Jordan could see me.

"My apologies Lt. Masters, how can I help you?" I asked.

"There's a crime scene on the lower east side, I need you to get to immediately, I will text you the details." Jordan stated.

"Damn it," I responded.

"ASAP, Sasha," she said with urgency.

"It's okay for you to address me as Sasha, but I can't address you as Jordan. You're too funny Jordan," I laughed and shook my head.

Jordan loved to be in control, and the moment a person was unable to control you, they became distant and acted as if you did something to hurt them, typical narcissist bullshit.

"Sasha, just crawl your ass off whatever dick or pussy you are on and be on your way," Jordan snorted. I can feel envy and hate through the phone.

"You're just mad it ain't you." I answered and disconnected the call before Jordan could respond.

"Duty calls?"

That was the voice of one of my ongoing flings, Savior.

"You already know. I think you better be getting home, I'm sure your wife is looking for you."

"Fuck her. How about you turn that ass over and let me get a taste before you run off to handle your business." Savior demanded.

"Hell, why not? That dead motherfucker ain't going anywhere." I said as I turned over, tooted my ass in the air and waited for Savior to do whatever the fuck he wanted. When he stuck his tongue in my ass, I knew what time it was.

Savior held my leg up and propped it over his shoulder. He ate me from the front to the back as I played with my pussy, but my patience was wearing thin, and I needed him to get this show on the road. I didn't want Jordan calling me back asking me where I was at.

"Savior, pick a hole and put that motherfucker in it! I HAVE TO GO!" I yelled.

"My pleasure," Savior said as he forced his dick in my ass.

I gasped when he entered me, because I liked the pain.

"Is this what you want?" Savior asked as he pumped in and out of me.

"Yes, daddy! Fuck me harder!" I said as I began to thrust my hips and ass back at Savior.

He grabbed a fist full of my hair and brought my face closer to his, before forcing his tongue down my throat.

I played with my clit as he punished my ass. The multiple orgasms I experienced when I had sex with Savior was enough to keep me wanting more. I knew he was a married man, but that wasn't my problem. I only wanted to see one side of him, the good side, she could deal with the rest.

Savior was almost six feet tall, with dark chocolate skin and snow-white teeth. He worked as a District Attorney in the Wayne County Courthouse for twenty-two years and was counting down the days he was able to retire. He hoped to live off his retirement on the sunny island of Aruba, but the chances of doing so were slim to none, if his wife had anything to do with it.

Savior shoved my head into the bed and positioned himself on top of me as he continued to punish my third hole.

"Just like that, daddy! Show me who's the boss." I said in the sexiest voice I could muster up.

Savior loved it when I talked dirty to him, it made his dick hard. I played with my clit until I started to climax.

"I'm about to cum, Savior," I announced as I pumped harder.

"Shit so am I! Tell daddy how much you love this dick!" Savior commanded.

"I love your dick, daddy. Cum for me. Cum all in my ass," I purred.

Unable to hold it any longer, Savior pumped several more times before cumming inside of my ass.

"Damn, you never disappoint Mr. Masters. Sometimes I wish I had you all to myself." I laughed as I made my way to the shower.

"No, you don't, Sasha. You're nowhere near wanting to settle down, you like too much of a variety," Savior said as he followed behind me.

Savior grabbed a wash towel and his toothbrush I kept for him in his bag in the bathroom drawer. Most of my indiscretions were done at hotels or at the homes of my flings. There were only a few who knew where I lived, and that's because we were somehow connected through work.

"Well, it sounded good. I guess you're not going to shower with me today?" I asked.

"I can't, I'm already going to have to hear her mouth when I get home," he said.

"Suit, yourself," I said as I continued to lather with my favorite Dove Lavender body wash.

Savior finished brushing his teeth and stuck his head inside of the shower for a kiss.

"I will talk to you later," he said after kissing me on the lips.

"Maybe,"

"Don't play with me Sasha," Savior said, giving me a stern look.

I don't know why he thought he could scold me like I was his child. He knew better than anyone that I hated to be contained or controlled.

"I will tell your wife, you said hi," I smiled.

"Yeah okay. I'm out," Savior said as cut his eyes at me and exited the bedroom.

*****

"Detective Grant, it's nice of you to show up. Late night date?" Jordan asked sarcastically.

"You know me better than anybody Lieutenant," I said, giving it right back to her.

Jordan and I had a love/hate relationship. She hated my attitude, and I loved to get under her skin.

"What do we have here?" I said looking at the taped off area in front of me.

"Older gentleman, headless, dickless, and of course, lifeless." Jordan said as she lifted the tape as we proceeded to the crime scene. I grabbed the pair of gloves hanging from my back pocket and put them on.

"I thought you said one victim, why do I see two sheets?" I asked.

Jordan pulled back the first sheet and exposed the man's head. His dick was stuffed inside of his mouth.

"Damn, he was definitely blessed with a big dick," I said with a smile on my face.

"Is dick the only thing you think about?" Jordan asked with an attitude.

"Of course not," I bit my bottom lip and eyeballed the honeypot in between Jordan's legs.

"Get your mind out the gutter and have more respect for the dead." She rolled her eyes and started surveying the area.

"My mind ain't in the gutter, and this motherfucker doesn't need respect, he needs a body bag." I corrected her as I pulled the other bloody sheet back and saw what was left of his mangled body.

"Damn, what in the hell did this to him?" I said out loud.

"A werewolf," I heard someone yell from above.

"Ma'am, there's no such thing as werewolves," I advised the nosey neighbor in the apartment above the crime scene.

"Maybe you're referring to a pack of dogs." I smiled at her gently.

"When was the last time you saw a dog stuff a man's penis in his mouth?" The older lady said with a hint of an attitude.

"You may have a point, but when was the last time you saw a werewolf roaming the streets of Detroit?" I countered.

"Last night," she replied before slamming her window closed.

I guess she didn't like my response. Looks like it's going to be a long night.

Chapter 5: Sting

I was sitting at home watching the 5 o'clock news with my daddy when the news anchor announced a breaking story.

"Early this morning Detroit police recovered the body of an unknown black male, who appeared to be in his mid-forties in an alley on Detroit's east side. Authorities say the man's head was completely severed from his body. One of the officers described the scene as gruesome and disturbing. We will update you with more of the story as it unfolds," said the news anchor, before tagging on her partner to discuss another story.

"That was right down the street!" Daddy shouted.

"How do you know? They didn't say where the body was located?" I quizzed my father.

Of course, I knew the murder scene was down the street, because I did it, but how did he know?

"I lived in this neighborhood all of my life, baby girl, I know that raggedy ass apartment anywhere."

My daddy was right. He knew this neighborhood like the back of his hand.

"Did the news anchor say his head was severed from his body?"

"Sounds like it," I responded.

"I'm sure he deserved it." My daddy said, taking me by surprise.

"You think so?"

"Hell yeah! When a motherfucker chops your fucking head off, it's personal. You either fucked with somebody's money or fucked with someone's property. Property meaning, someone's prize possession, like their wife, child, or mother."

"Would you kill somebody if they ever tried to hurt me?" I asked my daddy with a serious look on my face.

"Baby girl, I will kill a fucking brick over you, and you better do the same for me. We are all we got," My daddy said and kissed me on the forehead.

I fell into my daddy's arms and put my arms around his waist, like I used to do when I was a little girl.

"I will kill anybody that ever tried to hurt you daddy, I promise." I pledged to my daddy, meaning every word.

Thoughts of my mother tried to enter my head, but I blinked them away, along with the tears that tried to escape my eyes. I hadn't seen her since I was three years old. She was dead to me the moment I found out she left daddy and I behind. For the longest, it was my daddy, Dash, and I against the world, until I met Caesar.

******

The next morning, the word had spread around the neighborhood that Marvin was the man that was found mangled in the alley.

Aaron was sitting on the porch playing on his iPad.

"Hi, Aaron," I said as I walked across the street to be nosey.

"Hi Sierra!" he smiled.

"Is it true what everybody is saying? Was that your dad they found in the alley?" I asked.

"He wasn't my daddy, and yes it's true," Aaron's smile disappeared.

"My bad, I meant no disrespect. How is your mom taking it?" I asked.

"She's been crying all morning."

"She will get over it. He seemed like a sorry piece of shit if you ask me," I said, waiting for Aaron's response.

"Tell me about it. I'm glad he's dead," Aaron said with venom in his voice.

"You see, wishes really do come true," I smiled.

"Huh?" Aaron said with a look of confusion on his face.

"Never mind."

Dash walked by and gave me a holler.

"Hey Sting! Aaron!"

Aaron waved at Dash.

"I will check you out later, Aaron. Take care of your mother. You're the man of the house now." I advised him as I gave him dap and walked away with Dash.

"What's up Dash?" I asked as we walked down the street.

"Girl, somebody finally fucked Marvin's punk ass up, huh? Got his ass good," Dash said.

"I guess so," I said nonchalantly.

"Word on the street is that he was killed by a werewolf. Do you know anything about that?" Dashed eyed me suspiciously.

"Nope. You?" I countered.

"Nope."

A moment of silence went by before Dash continued.

"Look, I know after that whole Two Live Crew bullshit, you said you didn't want to be down with no crew, but I think you may like this one." Dash argued.

"Why can't we start our own crew?" I asked.

"We don't have the manpower. Ain't too many mafuckas checking for the gay boy. I already asked Caesar, and he's cool with it." Dashed assured me.

"Caesar? What kind of name is that?" I laughed as I noticed a group of people walking up the street. They were dressed in black and wore red, yellow, or green bandanas. This was the first time I saw a crew representing a variety of colors.

"That's the name of a God honey! Wait until you see him up close. His eyes are mesmerizing as fuck, too bad he ain't gay, because babbbyyyy!! Uh, uh, uh!!" Dash pranced around me.

Dash was so animated, and I loved him for it. Even in my darkest time, he could always put a smile on my face.

"I will think about it, but I don't want to make any promises," I informed Dash.

"Don't think too long, because that's them," Dash confirmed, pointing to the crew in front of us.

Seconds later, I was standing next to the finest guy I had ever seen. He was about six feet tall, with curly brown hair, with funny looking eyes. He looked like a young Snoop Dogg mixed with a little Nipsey. There were about six other members with Caesar, men, and women, but I only saw one person.

Ceasar was the leader of the newest crew on the scene called The Howling Huskies. Dash was right, after what Blaze and his friends had done to me, I could never be under his leadership, even with revenge on my mind. We disassociated ourselves from the Seven Mile Wolf Pack and hadn't looked back since.

"What up? You must be Sting?" Caesar said in a baritone voice.

"I am," I responded, mesmerized by Caesar's eyes.

"I'm Caesar, Dash said you wanted to be down with our crew, is that true?" he asked.

"That depends, what's the initiation process," I asked, thinking back to that dreadful day I asked Blaze the same question.

"We ain't with all that shit. It's all about honesty, loyalty, and respect. If you promise to be honest to the crew, loyal to the crew, and respect the crew, then you're in," Caesar answered.

"That won't be a problem, I can be very loyal," I answered, looking into Caesar's eyes.

"Is that right?" he asked, smiling at me, exposing a set of perfect white teeth, and one dimple on the left side of his cheek.

"Yes, very much so," I smiled back.

"I almost forgot, there was one more requirement," he said before his eyes shifted from green to a hazel color.

This was how werewolves informed each other they were werewolves as well. To a regular human it may appear so subtle that they may not notice the shifting of the eyes. I shifted my eyes from brown to black. Caesar smiled and sighed. It was almost as if he was relieved, he didn't have to turn me away.

Caesar and I shared a moment by shifting our eyes back and forth with one another. I refused to be the one to break the trance, but Dash put a stop to all of that.

"Uhmmm, I can be loyal too," Dash chimed in.

"My bad bro," Caesar laughed.

Caesar and Dash shared the same eye signal before Caesar shifted his attention to the both of us.

"It will be a full moon tonight. Let's meet in the middle of the woods where the moon shines brightest," Caesar instructed.

"Are we in or are we out!" Dash shouted.

Everybody laughed, including me.

"Relax, I will see y'all tonight." Caesar laughed as he and the crew walked away, leaving us with unanswered questions.

"What you think, bitch?" Dash asked.

"I think I need to go home and find something to wear for tonight!" I danced.

"Bitch! It's the fucking woods, you ain't trying to be dressed up for nobody, but Caesar. I saw y'all shifting eyes back and forth at one another," Dash checked me.

"What if I am? He's sexy than a motherfucker," I added.

"See, I told you this new crew was going to be dope. Fuck Seven Mile Wolf Pack, we're the Howling Huskies hoes!" Dash yelled in the middle of the street for the entire block to hear.

"Unofficially. After tonight, we will be official like a referee with a whistle, bitch!" I danced as I gave Dash five.

"Okay girl, let me go find something to wear as well. One of them fine ass niggas in the crew may dabble on the other side." Dash said as he sashayed up the block to Kris's house.

Chapter 6: Caesar

After meeting with Dash and Sting, Dame and I decided to hit the mall to get fresh for tonight's festivities. Dame, my right-hand man, and I walked back to my house to get the car and head to the mall. Usually, I wasn't so smitten by females, but Sting was different. She was exceptionally beautiful with her mocha brown skin, long braids, and slim-thick frame. When I looked in her eyes, I felt an instant connection.

"Dame, do you believe in love at first sight?"

"You must be talking about Sting," Dame laughed.

"Nigga, is it that obvious?" I asked.

"Fuck yeah! You motherfuckers were shifting eyes back and forth and shit. You ain't never did that shit with any of the other ladies in the crew," Dame stated.

"Nobody has ever captured my attention like Sting. I don't know what it was, but I felt something I'd never felt before," I confessed.

"Calm down, Superfly. You don't want to fall head over heels and get your feelings hurt. You don't even know if shorty has a man or not," Damn responded.

I could always count on Dame to give it to me raw and uncut. That's why he was my right-hand man.

"You're right, dog, let me pump my brakes. But if shorty has a man, she about to dead that shit, because I plan on making her my queen," I manifested my feelings to Dame.

"I hear you, Cease, but give the girl some air, she hasn't officially crossed over yet, damn," Dame said as he turned up the radio in my black-on-black Durango.

I let the sounds of Moneybagg Yo's *If Pain Was a Person* bump as we headed up seventy-five north to Somerset Mall. The lyrics to this song hit home in so many ways. Motherfuckers were out here unloyal as fuck. I've seen so many people come and go. It's true what they say, everybody ain't built for this game called life. Thankfully I knew how to weed out the real from the fake.

Dame and I stepped out of my truck and walked inside Macy's. I didn't have a lot of money for designer shit and wasn't scared to admit it. Give me a Polo outfit and some fresh Air Force Ones, and I am straight.

I hope Sting isn't one of those superficial, on the surface, females whose entire life was built on what they wear and which social media site to post it on.

Two hours later, Dame and I were walking out of the mall with a brand-new pair of gym shoes and four bags of clothes from Macy's, and various stores.

"What's your honest opinion of allowing Dash into the crew?" I asked.

"I don't give a fuck. Who he's fucking ain't my concern. The only thing I care about is if the motherfucker is honest, loyal, and respectful to our crew." Dame answered.

"I'm with you, bro. I don't give a fuck who he is laying pipe to or who's laying pipe to his ass. It just better not be Sting," I smiled.

"Here your ass goes! Pussy whipped before you get the pussy," Dame shook his head and laughed.

"Man, fuck that. I'm claiming her now. Closed mouths don't get fed," I informed him.

Dame and I bopped our heads as we headed back to the hood to get ready for tonight's event. I was looking forward to seeing Sting tonight. I hoped that the feelings were mutual, and she was willing to be the queen to my king.

*****

The crew and I headed towards the woods about thirty minutes before the sun started to set. I delegated the ladies of the crew, Layla and Tinkle, the task of purchasing a few decorations, and buying food and alcohol. I wanted to make everything perfect for Sting, and Dash.

We started the ceremony once Dash and Sting arrived. She was dressed in a form fitted Tommy Hilfiger dress, with matching slides. Her braids were pulled up in a pineapple bun with a few strands hanging down. Sting wore no makeup, just a heavy coat of sparkly lip gloss. She looked good enough to taste. Dash had on a pair of khaki cargo shorts with a white undershirt beneath a bright yellow button up, and a pair of khaki boat shoes.

I grabbed Sting by the hand and walked her deeper inside the woods to have a private conversation.

"You look really pretty, Sting," I complimented her.

"You can call me Sierra," she said shyly.

"That's a pretty name, you look like a Sierra," I smiled.

"How do a 'Sierra' look?" she asked.

"Gorgeous," I answered.

"Good answer, Mr. Caesar,"

"Do you have a man, Sierra?"

"I'm between men at the moment,"

"Not anymore," I said as I walked closer to her.

"You don't even know me," she responded.

"I will get to know you as we go. I'm not taking no for an answer," I said with all seriousness.

"That's good, because I wasn't going to tell you no," Sierra said as she placed her arms around my neck and kissed me on my lips softly.

I cupped her ass and kissed her back hard. My dick was so hard, that I was poking Sierra in the stomach with it. She looked down at my dick protruding through my joggers and licked her lips.

"I can't wait to bounce on that motherfucker," She cooed.

"You think you can handle all this dick? It's not even at its full potential," I teased.

"Oh, I can handle it, just make sure it's all mine to handle, because I don't share dicks," she threatened.

"Baby, you don't have to threaten me, I'm all yours. Loyalty, honor, and respect, remember?" I assured her.

"Good, because if you ever give my dick to anybody else, I will bite that motherfucker off and stuff it in your mouth," Sierra said in a menacing tone.

"Baby girl, when I get a hold of your ass, you're going to be begging me to keep this dick in your mouth," I said as I cupped her ass bringing her closer to me, pressing my dick further in her stomach.

She cooed, took my hand, and placed it between her legs. Sierra didn't have any panties on, and her hairless pussy was wet as fuck. Two of my fingers slid inside of her pussy with no effort. She closed her eyes and grinded against my fingers. Unable to take it anymore, I removed my fingers and pulled my dick out of my Polo jogger shorts. Usually, I strapped up when I fucked, but because she was my woman, and future wife, I wasn't dumbing her pussy down by using no fucking condom.

I lifted Sierra up and positioned her on the top of the head of my dick, and she slid down slowly. Her tight pussy swallowed my dick, instantly.

"Ooohhhh! This dick feels so good!" she confessed as she started to buck wildly.

"It's all yours baby, ride this dick," I instructed as I lifted her up and down on my dick.

I fought hard not to cum until she got hers off, but she felt so good. I closed my eyes and looked away from Sting to try to prevent from cumming first.

"I'm about to cum, Cease," Sierra announced.

"Cum on this dick baby," I said as I bounced her up and down harder. Sting's titties bounced up and down in her dress, before her entire body started to shake, and she came all over my dick.

I tried to wait for her to catch her breath, because I still hadn't got off yet.

"Put me down," Sierra demanded.

I did what she asked of me and watched as she walked over to a nearby tree and bend over.

"Get your ass over here and fuck the shit out of me, daddy." Sierra commanded as she hiked up her dress exposing her bare ass.

I smiled and stroked my dick as I walked over, never taking my eyes off her glistening pussy that was dripping with her cum. Unable to resist, I fell to my knees and stuck my extra-long tongue in Sierra's pussy and massaged her insides. One of the perks of being a werewolf was having an extra-long tongue and dick. Over the course of time, I learned how to control my transformation the way I wanted. I could transform my upper body into werewolf without transforming my lower body, I could expose my canine teeth without transforming my entire face. Right now, I only needed my tongue so I could devour Sierra's pussy and savor her juices.

I stuck my five-inch tongue inside of Sierra's pussy and fucked her as I fingered her clit. Sting gripped the tree and howled as my tongue went in and out of her pussy.

"Oh my God!! I can't take it, please stop!" She begged, trying to get away from me.

I stuck my nails in her thighs and held on to her firmly. Her body shook and she came in my mouth and squirted on the tree.

I released her shaking body and she fell to the ground. I used my werewolf strength and picked her up with one hand. I bent Sierra over a large tree stump and entered her from behind roughly causing her to howl out in pain and pleasure. When her body shook, I knew she was cumming again. I pumped in and out of Sierra as her nut dripped off my tongue onto the small of her back.

I growled as her ass jiggled when my body collided with hers. She was howling so loud, I'm sure the others heard her. To shut her up, I grabbed her by her neck and stuck my tongue inside her mouth. Sierra sucked my tongue as I fucked the wolf shit out of her and pressed my finger against her clit. When she tried to release my tongue so she could howl, I forced it further down her throat, causing her to gag, because I was tickling her tonsils.

Using my abilities to control every muscle in my body I increased the length of my dick by three inches and the width by two inches as my dick rested inside of her, causing her to cum instantly. Sierra was not able to control her transformation like I was. The excitement became too much to handle, and her bones started protruding, letting me know she was about to turn into a full-blown werewolf. To stop the transformation, I had to pull my dick out of her immediately.

"What the fuck you stop for? Put it back in!" she yelled with an attitude.

"I need you to calm the hell down; you're transforming," I informed her.

"So!" she yelled as she exposed her canine teeth, grabbed my dick, and tried to put it back inside of her.

"No, calm the fuck down, and I will give you all the dick you want." I teased her as I stroked my dick, to increase it another inch.

Sierra clearly didn't like being teased, because her face transformed as she growled, and tackled me to the ground. She removed her dress and positioned herself on top of my dick, making it disappear inside of her. I laid there in shock as Sting rode my dick like she was in a rodeo. She rocked her hips back and forth and up and down as she fucked the shit out of me. She bent down and we were eye to eye. She opened her mouth and let out a monstrous roar that made my eyelashes and the hair in my nose curl.

"Don't ever deny me of your body, again!" she roared.

I was so turned on her aggression, I instantly came. Sierra got off me and sucked me until I was bone dry and limp.

"Damn girl, do you have anger problems? You almost killed me." I said half-jokingly.

"Don't ever put that big motherfucker in me and not follow through," she said as she got dressed.

"Yes ma'am," I responded, and placed my dick back inside of my joggers, and brushed myself off from the access dirt on my clothes from when Sierra tackled me.

"Let's get back to the crew. I'm sure they're wondering where we are at." Sierra said as she started walking through the woods.

"With your big ass mouth, I'm sure they know exactly where we're at and what we were doing," I laughed.

"Shut up, before I strip your ass down to nothing and fuck you again," she warned.

"You got one up on me, but next time, it's all me," I said as I slapped her ass and watched it jiggle.

Damn, I can't wait until this meeting is over. I'm going to take her ass back to the crib and fuck the shit out of her.

Chapter 7: Sting

By the time Caesar and I made it back to the middle of the woods, the entire crew was there. They obviously heard me howling in the back of the woods and were doing a terrible job of trying disguise it. There was an awkward silence as everybody avoided making eye contact with Caesar and me; until Dash opened his big ass mouth.

"I guess I will ask the question, that us hoes are waiting to know. Bitch, was it good?"

Layla and Tinkle waited with listening ears for an answer. The guys weren't so obvious, but they were looking for any hint of satisfaction or dissatisfaction from Caesar. He stood stone faced and expressionless as everybody stared at me for an answer.

"Let's just say, that if any of you bitches ever think about touching my man in an inappropriate way, it's off with your motherfucking head," I said, pointing to Caesar.

Everybody laughed, the men guys gave each other dap, and the girls and Dash high fived each other, but I was dead fucking serious. I don't know what was in Caesar's dick, but it was lethal as fuck, and I couldn't wait until this ceremony is over so I could jump on that pogo stick all night long, and of course get to know him a little bit more.

"Can I have everybody's attention!" Caesar roared.

Everybody stopped what they were doing and turned their attention to Caesar.

"I would like you all to give a roaring howling for the two newest members of The Howling Huskies Dillan "Dash" Chavers and Sierra "Sting" Jacobs." Caesar announced.

"My last name is Matthews," I corrected Caesar.

"For now." Caesar responded.

We exchanged smiles and Caesar pulled me in close.

"OOOOOHHHHHHWHOOOOOOOOOO!"
Caesar yelled.

"OOOOOHHHHHHWHOOOOOOOOOO!"   All
the members yelled in unison.

Caesar clapped and everybody followed and gave
Dash and I a massive applause. Dash and I gave each other
a hug. It felt so good to be wanted and loved by someone
other than my father. Over a short period of time, Dash
became the brother I never had, and I loved him so fucking
much. I felt a tug on my arm and looked around and saw
the beautiful eyes of Caesar staring at me. I let go of Dash
and fell in the arms of my man.

Caesar brought his lips to mine, and we shared a
passionate kiss.

"Do you believe in love in first sight?" I asked
Caesar after I broke our kiss.

Caesar threw his head back and laughed.

"What's so funny?" I asked, feeling stupid that I had even brought it up.

"I asked Dame the same thing earlier," Caesar confessed.

My smile reappeared as I swayed back and forth in Caesar's arms to the music that was now playing from someone's phone.

"So, you feel the same way as I do?" I quizzed Caesar.

"Absolutely," he responded.

"Good, because I don't want to be in this alone," I answered, sincerely.

"As long as I'm alive Sierra, you don't ever have to worry about being alone again," Caesar said as he lifted my chin and kissed me softly on my lips. I grabbed his bottle lip and bit down hard, drawing blood. Caesar touched his lip with the tip of his fingers. I grabbed his bloody finger, placed it in my mouth and sucked it. I watched as blood dripped down his lip onto his chin before I licked the blood away and sucked his bloody lip.

"I'm going to hold you to every word Mr. Jacobs," I threatened Caesar.

"You better," Caesar responded.

Everybody was dancing, drinking, and having a great time. The moon was bright, and we were waiting for Caesar to give a sign that it was time to transition. Out of nowhere we heard a thunderous clap. We all stopped dancing and looked in the direction of where the clapping was coming from. Blaze and the rest of the Seven Mile Wolf Pack were standing in front of us. This was the closest I had been to Blaze since the day he and the crew violated me.

"What are you doing here?" Caesar pushed me to the back with the other women. The men stepped forward and stood along the side of Caesar.

"Hey, Sting. Long time, no see." Blaze said as he peeked his head around Caesar and addressed me.

Caesar pushed Blaze backwards causing him to stumble.

"Motherfucker if you ever address my woman again, I will break every bone in your fucking body." Caesar yelled.

"Calm down, she doesn't mind being passed around the crew," Slime laughed, causing a ripple effect of laughter within his crew.

"You're a motherfucking lying ass son of a bitch! My friend ain't no fucking hoe! You nasty motherfuckers," Dash screamed.

"Dash! Enough," I yelled, stopping him from telling the truth about what happened to me that dreadful night in the warehouse.

"I advise you to leave while you're still able to stand," Caesar threatened Slime and the rest of the crew.

Slime tried to rush Caesar, but Dame was on it and jumped in front of him.

"We won't ask you motherfuckers to leave again," Dame said in a threatening voice.

"We will leave, but this isn't over, right, Sting? Remember, you will always be mine," Blaze stated as he and his crew walked away.

"I wish somebody kill them shiesty motherfuckers," Layla stated.

"Your wish is my command," Dash responded in a low tone.

Caesar watched until Blaze and his crew were no longer in sight. I grabbed his hand, hoping he didn't pull away from me.

"Are you going to tell me what that was about?" he asked me without looking.

"Yes, when time permits," I answered.

"Good, because I need to know what the hell is going down before I kill that motherfucker and his crew," Caesar responded.

The crew tried to keep the party going, but the mood was killed. Feeling depleted, we packed up everything and headed home.

"You're coming with me tonight," Caesar demanded.

"Okay." I answered and followed closely behind him.

*****

We arrived at Caesar's apartment within minutes of the woods. I had never noticed these apartments before because they were discreetly hidden behind a restaurant and a gas station. I could tell Caesar was upset because he didn't say one word.

He opened the door to the apartment and allowed me to walk in first. Wasting no time, he went in straight for the questions.

"What's going on Sierra? What was Blaze and his crew talking about?" Caesar asked.

I grabbed Caesar by his hand and led him over to his couch to sit down. I took a deep breath because I felt the tear forming in the ducts of my eyes. This would be the first time I talked about the rape since it happened.

"Before I asked to join your crew, I was a member of Seven Mile Wolf Pack. Blaze and four of the men of the crew, asked me to meet them at an abandoned warehouse later that day to be initiated. I should have known something was wrong," I said as I started to cry.

Caesar scooted closer and put his arm around me.

"I know it's hard, baby, but I need for you to finish telling me the story," Caesar said softly.

I laid my head on his chest and told him the rest of the story.

"Blaze instructed me to take off my clothes, but I couldn't move. He ripped off my clothes and he raped me, and so did the others. When I tried to scream, he told one of the other guys to put my shirt in my mouth! They all took turns raping me!" I cried hysterically.

Caesar didn't say anything, he just held me closer and tried to console me as I cried like a baby. It felt good to let it out and tell somebody besides Dash.

"I'm so sorry that happened to you, Sierra. It was not your fault." Caesar said as he sniffled.

"There's one more thing I need to tell you. Promise you won't hate me or leave me." I turned to him and begged.

"Sierra, I told you that you don't have to worry about that," Caesar said with anger and tears in his eyes.

"Promise me!" I cried as I wrapped my arms around his neck.

I was so scared that Caesar wouldn't want me that I didn't want to let him go.

"Sierra, you're freaking me out. Baby, I promise I won't hate you or leave you. Finish telling me what happened," he said calmly.

"Shortly after I was raped, I found out I was pregnant with Blaze's baby. I got an abortion," I added.

"How do you know it was Blaze's baby, if all the guys did that to you?" he asked.

I could tell he was avoiding using the "r" word.

"The other guys sodomized me. Blaze had done the same thing you did with your dick. He made it bigger than it was. One of the other guys attempted to enter after Caesar but I guess Blaze had stretched me out," I looked down ashamed.

"Are you saying that Blaze is a werewolf too?" Caesar questioned.

"Not only did he impregnate me, but he also turned me into a hybrid werewolf as well," I cried.

Caesar jumped up and started pacing the room, he was furious. I got scared he would leave, so I jumped up and wrapped my arms around him.

"Please forgive me, I'm so sorry, I knew I shouldn't have gone!" I fell to Caesar's knees and cried.

Caesar pried me off him and sat on the floor next to me.

"Sierra, none of it was your fault. I need you to forgive yourself baby. The only person that is going to be sorry is Blaze and his crew," Caesar stated.

"I pray to God, one day they will get what's coming to them!" I threatened.

"Say less." Caesar said as his eyes shifted.

Caesar picked me up and carried me to his bedroom. He removed my clothes, laid me down and kissed me from head to toe. Afterwards he lifted both of my legs and kissed the inside of my thighs. I laid on my back and thought about all the hurt and pain I dealt with in the short time I've been on this earth. I constantly asked God why me.

Would this all have happened if my mother had been in my life? Her love was the love I had longed for all these years. She was the reason why I looked for love in the streets.

"Relax baby, let me make you feel good." Caesar said as if he had read my mind.

I took a deep breath and tried to enjoy Caesar's tongue darting in and out of my pussy. But the tears started to flow, and I couldn't stop them.

When he sucked on my clit, I cried out and arched my back. His tongue felt so good I pushed his head further inside of me. Caesar sucked, licked, and slurped until I exploded inside of his mouth. He climbed on top of me and kissed me as his finger alternated between my pussy to my clit, causing me to climax again before he entered me, and made love to me.

I kissed Caesar deeply as he stroked me long and hard, causing shock waves to be sent through my body.

"I love you, Caesar," I cried out.

"I love you too, Sierra. I promise nobody will ever hurt you again." Caesar promised.

Caesar positioned himself behind me, entered me slowly, and made love to me so good, I lost count of how many times I orgasmed. I held on tight and enjoyed all of him as he took me back and forth to ecstasy. I prayed he would always be there for me like I prayed for my daddy and Dash every night. I wouldn't know what to do if I ever lost either of them.

Chapter 8: Dash

The clouds covered the moon for a moment before they passed through like thieves of the night. I waited until everybody dispersed before I transitioned to a werewolf and headed in the direction Blaze and his crew went. I knew in a matter of time, they would split up, and I planned on making an example out of one of their asses when they did. They walked the streets like they hadn't raped and terrorized motherfuckers along the way. If they raped Sting, I was for certain they did it to others.

Blaze and the crew split up and disappeared down various streets. I chose Thor because he walked down a secluded area with several blown streetlights. He was live on Facebook talking shit about our crew and how Seven Mile Wolf Pack had punked us, so he wasn't paying attention when I crept up behind him.

"Fuck them punk motherfuckers! We got something for The Howling Huskies the next time we see their asses in the streets, no cap! Their leader, Caesar, is the biggest pussy of them all! That's why Seven Mile Wolf Pack ran through his bitch! That nigga doesn't know he is cuffing a whole hoe!" Thor laughed as he talked about Sting.

I growled as I crept up behind him on all fours and waited for him to turn around.

"Oh shit!" he screamed before he took off running.

I let him get a head start before I took off and raced behind him. Clearly Thor wasn't a werewolf, because if he was, he would've transitioned and fought me wolf to wolf. There was no way my gay ass was going to fight him man to man because I was not a fighter. That was one of the main reasons I became a werewolf, because it gave me power. When Sting found out she was a werewolf, she made me promise not to tell anyone. I advised her that the only way I would keep her secret is if she turned me into a werewolf as well.

Sting and I drove home in silence after I picked her up from the abortion clinic. I didn't know what to say but had to say something because the silence was killing me. Like usual, I said the dumbest shit a motherfucker can say to someone after they just killed their unborn child.

"Are you okay?"

Sting looked at me and rolled her eyes.

"Sorry, I don't know what to say." I confessed.

"It's okay Dash, it's not your fault," Sting stated.

I decided not to say anything, because I didn't want to stick my foot in my mouth again. Instead, I decided to turn up the radio. Latto's Put It on the Floor Again was on radio, so I started rapping with the music.

'Rip me out the plastic, I been acting brand new.

Bitches acting like they runnin shit, they really ran through.

I'll spend that 500, before I ever trap you.

I started dancing and singing in my seat as Latto rapped her part. Sting couldn't help but laugh at me and my dramatics. By the time Cardi's part came on, I had ripped Sting out the plastic too, and she started rapping.

'Put a ribbon on me, I been acting brand new.

I ain't smoking no za, lil bitch, I'm smoking on you...'

We both rapped the entire song as we drove down Eight Mile Road. By the time the song was over, Sting was back to her regular self. We laughed so hard; we were crying tears. Mine were happy tears, I wasn't so sure about Sting's.

"Dash, I know I thanked you so many times before, but I want to thank you again for saving my life." Sting said as she wiped the tears away.

"You don't have to thank me. I'm just glad that you were okay," I smiled and blew her kiss.

"I need to tell you something," she said.

"Okayyyy, spill it bitch!" I said, animated per usual.

"I'm a werewolf," Sting responded.

I stopped the car in the middle of traffic and jumped out, screaming. Sting jumped out of the car and started chasing after me.

"Get away from me! Help! Help! She's trying to kill me! Help! Help!" I screamed.

"Dash, calm down! Nobody is trying to kill you, get back in the car," Sting screamed.

"Uh uh, bitch! You're not about to eat me!"

"Will you calm the fuck down, and get in the fucking car?" Sting yelled.

"You promise, bitch?"

"I promise!" Sting yelled.

"Pinky swear?"

"I pinky swear, bitch! Get in the car!" Sting laughed as she screamed at me.

Cars were honking like shit at me.

"Fuck y'all! None of you mafuckas ain't even try to help me!" I yelled at the motorist and gave them the finger before getting back in the car cautiously.

Sting busted out laughing.

"I really needed that laughed."

"Bitch, are you fucking serious? You're a werewolf?" I asked.

"Yes," she answered in between laughs.

"How?"

Sting informed me it happened the night Blaze raped her, and he was the one that turned her into a werewolf when he ejaculated inside of her and got her pregnant. I asked her so many questions, and she answered each one of them patiently. When she told me she had gained extreme strength, I was sold.

"I want to be a werewolf too." I informed Sting.

"Bitch, I don't think so, this shit is not all fun and games. Sometimes I can't control when I transform, and it's painful as fuck!" Sting added.

"I don't give a fuck! You said you have the strength of ten men, bitch I barely have the strength of ten babies! I need muscles, I don't care if they only come out during a full moon," I added.

"Why don't you think about it for a while." Sting tried to talk me out of it,

"I thought about it, let's do it!" I said excitedly.

"Overnight, Dash. Think about it overnight, do some research for yourself. If you want me to bite the shit out of you afterwards, then I will do it." Sting conceded.

Sting was surprised I still wanted to be a werewolf after the twenty-four-hour period. She still refused to "turn" me, until I told her I would expose her if she didn't. I guess she figured if we were both werewolves, then it would be 'our' secret to keep, so the bitch bit me, hard!

I didn't notice anything different at first. One foggy night, Sting led me into the woods and advised me to take off my clothes. At first, I thought she was trying to fuck me, because everybody wanted to try the gay guy. The moment I saw the full moon, I knew exactly why we were here.

The transition was painful as fuck. Whiskers and bones protruding out of my face, body, and the muscles! Babyyyy, I had muscles for days. I strutted around the woods doing my best Hulk Hogan impression. I lost plenty of clothes not knowing how to control when and how I transitioned, but things have gotten a lot easier.

I pounced on Thor's back, when he fell to the ground and his phone flew out of his hand. I ripped his shirt off his back spinning him around, so we were face to face. His live was still streaming on his phone, but I ignored it and straddled him.

"What the fuck?" Thor asked.

"Who's the punk bitch now? All you motherfuckers are going to pay for what you did to Sting." I threatened.

"Sting? Is this what the fuck this is all about? A bitch?" Thor said.

My werewolf nails emerged from my real nails, and I slapped his lips off his face. He felt for his lips with his hands, but they were no longer there. He started mumbling something, but I couldn't understand him because he didn't have any lips!

I started windmilling the shit out of him.

What the fuck am I doing? I'm a fucking werewolf, not a lil bitch!

I grabbed a hold of Thor's neck and tugged as his flesh ripped inside of my mouth. My teeth caught hold of Blaze's Adam's apple. I pulled hard until I ripped it out of his throat. Blood squirted everywhere as Thor choked and reached for his neck.

I ripped off his limbs one by one until there was nothing attached to his torso, but his head. His lifeless eyes looked at me as blood continued to squirt from every hole that was exposed. I stepped over his phone, leaving a bloody print on his phone, and I walked down the deserted street. Feeling good about my first kill, I howled and disappeared into the darkness.

Chapter 9: Sasha Grant

Today was a long fucking day. I spent the entire day surveying the alley where that man's body was found, badly mutilated. According to his I.D., his name was Marvin Salis, and he lived not too far away from the crime scene. I went into the office for a moment to drop evidence, and to write up the report. Jordan was staring at me from the other side of the room.

"Can I help you?" I said to Jordan without looking up.

"Oh, I can't look at you now?" she asked with an attitude.

"No." I responded as I gathered my things and walked past Jordan on my way out of the door.

I had nothing against Jordan, but she had a problem with me. She tried to control me because she was unable to control her household, but I wasn't having it. Every chance

I got, I gave her back the same energy she'd given me, in and out of the office. Personally, I think she got off on it.

I drove home in silence thinking about what or who could have done so much damage to that man. If it wasn't for his I.D., we would not have been able to identify him.

Loud music from the car on the side of me caught my attention. A car full of teenage girls was dancing to Glorilla's *F.N.F. Let's Go*. They all jumped out of the car and started twerking in front of the car and screaming "Let's Go!" I started bobbing my head to the catchy tune, before cars started honking. The teenagers jumped back inside of their car, peeled off, and I turned onto my block.

I pulled into my driveway and pressed the open button on my car garage opener. After I pulled my car inside the garage, I walked inside and dropped everything on the kitchen counter, grabbed a glass from the dishrack, and opened the bottle of Hennessey that I kept on the counter. I poured a double shot and drank it straight before I headed to the shower.

I tried to think of something other than the case I was working on but couldn't. Every time I closed my eyes, I saw what was left of the victim sprawled out in an alley. I lathered my body and allowed the hot water to sting my body and wash away all of today's woes. Ten minutes later, I grabbed my Terry cloth robe, and a body of baby oil and headed to my room.

I oiled my body down as I watched the news. A picture of the victim flashed across the tv screen before they showed a picture of a woman, whom I assumed was Marvin's wife crying her eyes out as a young boy stood by her emotionless. I turned the channel until I came across something I was familiar with, a rerun of *Good Times*. I laughed as JJ strutted like a skinny peacock, as Thelma and Michael roasted him, before my doorbell rang.

Who the hell is showing up to my house unannounced at this time of the night?

I looked out my peephole and sighed deeply. Seeing Jordan and Savior at my door only meant one thing, it was about to go down. I closed my robe and tied it tightly before I opened the door.

"What are y'all doing here?" I asked them.

He grabbed me by my face and kissed me deeply while she closed the door behind them. I ripped off his clothes as he untied my robe and threw it on the ground. In my peripheral, I could see her removing her clothes, then heading towards us. She turned my face to hers and forced her tongue down my throat.

Per usual, she took control and pushed me down on the couch before dropping to her knees and disappearing between my legs. She licked and sucked my pussy like it was the best thing she had tasted since forever.

"Ooooohhh Jordan, suck my pussy," I cooed as I tried to push her head inside of me.

He positioned himself on the side of me and stroked his dick in my face. I licked my tongue out to welcome his dick, and he obliged by placing it on my tongue, so the wetness of my mouth can guide it down my throat.

He held onto the back of my head as he slid his dick in and out of mouth. Jordan stuck two fingers inside my pussy as she slurped and alternated between my pussy lips and clit. I grinded on her fingers as she fucked me fast and hard causing me to cum inside of her mouth. After she was done, she pushed her husband out of the way and stuck her tongue inside of my mouth so I could taste myself.

I felt another set of familiar lips on my pussy, and they felt just as good as the last. I removed my mouth from Jordan and looked down at his head buried in between my legs, eating the fuck out of my pussy.

"Yesssss Savior, eat that pussy, baby," I demanded as Jordan positioned her pussy

on my face.

I spread her legs, parted her pussy lips with my tongue and flicked her clit. Jordan shivered each time I repeated the process. She rode my face as my tongue darted in and out of her wet pussy. As Savior licked and sucked me, Jordan played with my clit. It was like we were both in a race to see who can make who cum the fastest. Determined not to lose, I pulled her closer to me, sucked on her clit a little harder and spread her ass cheeks further apart, by placing one finger from each hand inside of her, causing her to cum hard inside of my mouth. I licked and sucked her clit until she came again and again, before she eventually rolled over and tapped out.

I was determined to get my nut off, so I climbed on top of her face and started to ride her. Savior stood behind me and licked my pussy from the back, before he slid his dick inside of my ass and started to fuck me.

The friction of Jordan's tongue, and Jordan's dick sent me into overdrive, and I bucked against Savior with force. Savior picked me up with his dick still inside of my ass and sat on the couch, as I straddled him. Jordan crawled over on all fours and positioned herself back in between my legs.

I grabbed her by her hair and mushed her face inside of my pussy as I rode the shit out of Savior's dick.

"Ride that dick bitch!" Savior demanded as he fingered me, leaving Jordan without anything to do.

Jordan removed Savior's dick from my ass and put it inside of her mouth, making Savior go crazy.

"Oh shit! What the fuck!" Savior said as Jordan slurped my ass juice off his dick.

Jordan continued to suck his dick until he was about to cum. She removed his dick from his mouth and sucked his balls. I positioned myself on Savior's face and let him eat me out like only he and his wife could while I held onto the back of his head. Jordan gave my ass a hard slap before she positioned herself on her husband's dick and rode it as she fucked my ass with her tongue. I was in lustful heaven and felt an eruption coming on.

"Ooohhh, I'm about to cum!" I announced.

Savior mumbled and bounced Jordan up and down on his dick faster, as she moaned in pleasure. We all climaxed together and collapsed on separate sides of the couch.

"Fuck," I said out of breath as Jordan scooted downtown and licked me clean with her tongue. I grabbed Savior's dick, guided it to my mouth and sucked the rest of his babies out of him, before we cuddled on the couch and fell asleep.

Three hours later, we were awakened by the sound of Jordan's work phone. She looked at the caller ID before answering.

"Hello?" she responded in a sleepy voice.

I couldn't hear who was on the other end of the phone, so I listened.

"You got to be kidding me. Where?" she questioned.

"Okay, I will be right there. Don't touch anything." Jordan instructed as she got up and got dressed.

"Who was that?" I asked.

"There has been another murder, the same as the other one, badly mutilated," she responded.

"Are you serious?" I asked, ready to go to sleep.

"Yes, I will text you the details. I expect to see you there within thirty minutes," she demanded.

"Don't let me have to call you, Sasha," she threatened before kissing me on the lips.

Jordan kissed Savior on his lips as well.

"I will see you at home in a couple of hours, Mr. Masters. Have Sasha drop you off on the way," Jordan said before she walked out of the door.

"Looks like you have to go back to work, Ms. Grant," Savior smiled.

"I guess I do," I said as I attempted to get up to go wash my ass and get dressed.

"Not so fast. I have you all to myself and I'm about to take advantage of it."

Savior flipped me on my stomach, forced his dick inside of my pussy and doggy-styled me out of three more orgasms. I had to literally force myself to get off the couch and into the bathroom. On the way to the bathroom, I noticed all the cum stains on the couch.

"Zelle me some money so I can clean my couch, plus a little extra for keeping you and your marriage together," I said without looking back.

As I entered the bathroom, I heard the alert on my phone indicating money was deposited into my account. I smiled as I got into the shower and waited for Savior to join me.

Chapter 10: Caesar

Sierra fucked me up with the information she dropped on me. I knew something was up based on the shit Blaze and his crew said, but never would I have thought it was as bad as Sierra said it was. I couldn't imagine how she felt after everything she had been through. I know I haven't known her long, but I truly believe I have loved her from the first moment I saw her. As her man, it's my job to protect her, and going forward I plan to do just that, because shit was about to get crazy in the hood.

Word on the streets, werewolves or wolf-like creatures were the cause of the death of the man found in the alley. The cops didn't have any leads, or any suspects.

I wasn't sure how much of the information the police had or believed about the killing being werewolf related, but I knew that it was only a matter of time before somebody started probing around our den trying to connect the dots. I wasn't ready for that type of heat.

I informed Dame to round up the crew, except for Sierra for a mandatory meeting. A clap back was a must, and I didn't want Sting anywhere near it. She was too emotionally invested, and I didn't want to risk her getting too hot headed and throwing off the plan.

By the time I got to the woods, everybody was waiting for me.

"What's up everybody? I called y'all here to discuss the Seven Mile Wolf Pack, and how in the fuck are we going to get rid of their asses. They hurt somebody that I have really grown to love, and they got to go. Usually, I don't take shit personally, but when it comes to someone I care about, it's personal. So, I would understand if anybody wanted out," I informed the crew.

"How many motherfuckers are we talking about?" Layla asked.

"Five," I responded.

"Four", Dash corrected me.

122

I looked at him suspiciously.

"Four," I repeated.

"What's the plan?" Dame asked.

"Layla and Tinkle, I need y'all to follow Blaze. One of y'all take the day shift and the other one take the night shift. Watch his every move for the next forty-eight hours. If he shits, I want to know what color it is and what he had for dinner. Do y'all understand?" I growled.

"What about the rest of them punk motherfuckers?" Dash asked.

"We're going to take care of their asses first. To my understanding, Blaze is the only one that is a hybrid. After we take care of them motherfuckers, I will handle Blaze." I stated.

"No, I will handle Blaze," a voice said from behind.

Everybody turned around to see Sierra standing there, madder than a motherfucker.

"What's up baby?" I hugged and kissed her.

"Don't hey baby me. Y'all having a secret meeting, or something? What happened to honesty?" she asked.

"How the hell did you find out where we were at?" I asked Sierra.

"Dash and I have each other's location,"

I looked at Dash in disbelief.

"What can I say, that's my best friend," Dash smiled nervously.

"Come here, baby," I said as I grabbed Sierra by her arm and led her away from the crew.

"I don't want you involved in this bullshit, you have been through so much already," I said as I touched her face.

"I got to be a part of this, them motherfuckers raped me!" she cried.

"I know baby, but we have to be smart about this, trust me," I reassured her.

Sierra wasn't happy about it, but she bowed down and allowed me to take control. I pulled her into my arms and allowed her to cry silently on my chest.

*****

Layla and Tinkle walked Sierra to my apartment before they set out to do surveillance on Blaze. As we left the meeting, we spotted Slime and Duke walking down the street. When they noticed us, they took off running.

Dash took off running with me as we gave chase with Dame and two other Huskies following closely behind.

Slime darted through traffic, and in between houses. We would have been able to catch his ass if we transitioned, but it was daylight, and the risk of people seeing us as werewolves wasn't worth it.

"Damn, that nigga was fast as fuck," Dame huffed out of breath.

"Yeah, they were hauling ass like a motherfucker," I laughed.

"Nigga, that shit ain't funny!"

"My bad, dog, but that shit was funny," I chuckled.

"Whatever, nigga. I'm about to head out, I will catch up with your ass later," Dame said as he walked away.

"Peace," I shouted behind Dame's back.

"I'm out too," Dash co-signed, before yelling out to Dame.

"Yo Dame, wait up!"

I watched Dash as he jogged to catch up with Dame.

I walked home with a little pep in my step knowing that Sierra was in my apartment waiting for me.

Crystal Kinn-Tarver

Chapter 11: Sasha

I became close friends with The Masters after Jordan, and I went to the local bar to celebrate after solving a very publicized murder. Jordan got touchy feely and started grinding on me on the dance floor. Knowing where it could lead to, I advised Jordan it was time to go. I knew how messy shit could get and I had no intention of getting involved with my boss.

Jordan's car was in the shop, so I dropped her off at home after we both had one too many drinks. I had to use the restroom, so Jordan offered hers. When I opened the bathroom door, Jordan was standing there naked as the day she entered this world.

Her body was beautiful and illuminated by a dimly lit red light coming from a nearby bedroom. Before I could object, Jordan had her tongue down my throat and her hand under my skirt. At first, I tried to reject her advances, but she was persistent and thanks to her I was hot and bothered.

I grinded on her fingers as they slid in and out of my pussy. Jordan licked my earlobe and kissed and sucked on my neck as I closed my eyes and rode her finger until I climaxed. The feeling of someone else's presence made me open my eyes. A fine ass man with a body of an African God stood in front of me. His chiseled chest and cocoa brown skin were barely visible in the semi-darkness. I had to blink several times to make sure I wasn't imagining him.

He grabbed my hand and pulled me into his chest. Jordan got on her knees and placed my leg on her shoulder as she dove in and began to lick the cum that was running down the inside of my leg. I grabbed a fist full of her unkept hair and pushed her face inside of my pussy as the African God parted my lips with his tongue. Moments later, our tongue danced with each other as Jordan's tongue danced with my clit. I had done several threesomes before, but nothing as spontaneous as this one, and I loved it.

He guided my hand down his chest until I reached the shaft of his dick. Together we stroked his massive manhood as we breathed heavily into each other's mouth. Jordan pressed downed on my clit, and I came for a second time. She licked and slurped me as I stroked the head of his dick and played with the pre cum on my fingers.

"Can I taste you?" I whispered in his ear.

"Only if you let me taste you as well," he responded.

"What's your name?" I asked as I kissed his ear and licked his neck.

He placed his hand around my neck.

"Savior," he whispered as he blew in my ear, causing me to cum again in Jordan's mouth.

Jordan licked me dry then joined me and Savior. I kissed her before I made her kiss Savior so he could taste me as well. While they were both preoccupied, I fell to my knees and licked my lips when I got the first glimpse of Savior's beautiful, black dick. I opened my mouth like an anaconda, relaxed my throat muscles, and inhaled all his dick until his balls were touching my chin.

"Ughhh," he grunted as he held on to my head to stop me from moving.

I knew this tactic well. Men did this to stop themselves from cumming prematurely. I held my position, because I wasn't ready for the night to end without having a chance to taste it, let alone, ride it. I released his dick to give him a chance to recover and started to suck his freshly showered balls.

Savior guided his dick to my mouth, and I licked the head a few times before I placed it in my mouth and let the back of my throat do the rest. Savior grabbed the back of my head as he pumped in and out of my mouth. Jordan joined me on the floor, lifted my chin, and placed her hand on top of Savior's hand. Together they forced Savior's dick further down my throat, causing me to gag throughout the ordeal.

"Suck his dick, bitch. You like how it taste?" Jordan taunted me as she pushed my head down forcefully. She licked away the slob and the precum that escaped from the sides of my mouth as I choked on Savior's dick. I could feel my pussy muscles contracting and I knew another orgasm was on the rise. I grabbed Jordan's hand and guided it to my clit so she could finish the job.

"Savior, she's so fucking wet. I think she enjoy sucking your dick just as much as you enjoy getting your dick sucked," Jordan said as she fingered me until I exploded again. She moaned as she dipped her fingers in my pussy and put them in her mouth several times, before dipping her fingers inside of my pussy a final time, and placing them in Savior's mouth, causing him to moan in pleasure.

Savior lifted me up on his shoulders, slammed me against the wall and ate my pussy like it was his last meal. I could hear Jordan sucking his dick as he worked his tongue just as good as his wife did, maybe even better. I moaned and bucked against his face and his tongue darted in and out my pussy. He slipped his thumb in my ass, causing me to arch my back and cum in his mouth.

"Fucckkkk!" I yelled as he lifted me up further and stuck his tongue in my ass as he fingered my clit.

"Yes daddy, oohh!" I cooed as Savior licked me from ass to clit, repeatedly, before I grabbed his head and came again for the umpteenth time.

He carried me on his shoulders, to the bedroom with the dimly lit red light, bending at the entrance so I wouldn't hit my head. Savior dropped me on the bed causing me to bounce several times and land on my stomach. When I tried to turn over, he slapped me on my ass hard.

"Don't you dare," he threatened as he bent down and ate me from the back.

Out of my peripheral, I saw Jordan open the nightstand, grab a gold wrapped condom and hand it to Savior. He opened the wrapper as he continued to eat my ass. Jordan aligned her pussy with my face and mushed my face in her pussy as Savior slid inside of me.

Together we moaned, as we exchanged bodily fluids and fuck faces. The sound of our bodies smacking and moaning, could only be described as "macaroni in a pot" filled the air and intensified our lust making session.

When I placed a finger in Jordan's ass, a domino effect of climaxing began. She arched her back as I latched down on her clit and played with her pussy. I moaned as Savior pounded me harder as his balls slapped against my clit, repeatedly. He let out a loud groan as he pumped faster and harder. In unison, we all made a musical song with our bodies before we collapsed on top of each other and fell asleep in each other's arms. Hours later, Jordan was called into the office on another case, leaving Savior and me alone to enjoy each other. We exchanged business cards and the next night he showed up to my house uninvited for round two.

That was a year ago. I wasn't sure if she suspected Savior and I was sleeping together behind her back, but if she didn't ask, I was not going to tell.

*****

"Nice of you to join us, Detective Grant," Jordan said, back in bitch mode.

You wouldn't have known that just an hour ago that her and her husband was at my door making a fuck sandwich out of me.

"Long exhausting night. I had a couple of unexpected guests that demanded my undivided attention," I said sarcastically as I walked under the tape and put on a pair of plastic gloves.

Jordan ignored my comment.

"We have a young black male, looks to be in his early twenties. From the looks of it he was chased down and struck from the back before he was attacked," Jordan stated.

I looked down at what was left of the man's body. His limbs were scattered about and were lying in a pool of blood. This scene was more gruesome than the last.

"Watch your step!" Jordan yelled.

I looked down and saw what looked like a chewed-up piece of meat.

"What the fuck is that?" I yelled.

"His lips," Jordan answered.

I jumped back, causing her to laugh.

"Who the fuck would do something like this?" I asked out loud.

"Or what," Jordan said as she directed my attention to the victim's cell phone.

A bloody print that resembled a dog's paw was on the screen of the phone.

"That's either a large dog or a…," I paused.

"Werewolf." Jordan finished my sentence.

A crowd started to form, and Jordan rushed the crime scene investigators to process the scene.

I glanced at the crowd and saw a familiar face staring down at the crime scene. When he looked up, I hurriedly turned around and looked in the opposite direction.

What the hell is he doing here? I knew I should have chosen another division.

I busied myself with the crime scene before I pretended to look for evidence behind a few wooden crates. I took a deep breath and looked in his direction. He looked as good as he did almost twenty years ago, except he sported a black and gray beard, with a matching mustache. He was bald headed but looked sexy as ever with a freshly shaven head. He wore a pair of nicely fitted jeans and a white tank top that exposed a bush of salt and pepper hair. In the middle of his chest was a gold necklace with a cross. Butterflies danced in my stomach as I thought about the only man I had ever loved.

"Sasha! Where are you at?" Jordan called my name, scaring the shit out of me.

When I looked back over, he was no longer there.

Fuck, I hope he didn't see me or hear Jordan call my name.

"Coming!" I called out as I reappeared from behind the crates.

"Let's go talk to the neighbors. I'm sure somebody heard something," Jordan instructed.

"Sounds like a plan," I said as I looked around to see if he was still around.

"Who are you looking for?" Jordan asked.

"Nobody, I will take this side of the street; you do the other," I said, changing the subject.

"Uhmmm, cool. It shouldn't take long, considering there's only about eight houses on the block," she laughed as she walked away.

Lord, I know we don't talk much, but please don't let him live in one of these houses, I beg of you.

I took a deep breath, knocked on the door, and hoped God was kind enough to hear my prayer.

I knew I had to come face to face with my past one day, but I didn't want it to be like this.

Chapter 12: Dash

He pulled me close, and I felt his dick poke me in my back. He kissed the back of my neck before he grabbed my dick and stroked it until it was erect. I moaned at his touch, grabbed his dick and placed it near the opening of my ass. He lubricated his hand with spit, then stroked his dick as he readied himself to enter me. I gasped as his dick stretched my opening and invaded my space.

"Baby, your dick feels so fucking good," I cooed.

"Not as good as your ass feel, throw that ass back on a nigga's dick," he said as he grabbed my hips and rocked them back and forth. I lifted my leg high to the ceiling, and twerked my ass against his dick, making him go crazy.

"Ooohh, just like that, fuck this dick, baby," he said in between moans.

"Whose dick is that daddy?" I asked as I grinded on his dick, as he stroked me.

"It's yours, baby," he responded as he bit his bottom lip.

"Whose ass is this? he asked as he gripped my dick and stroked it harder.

"It's yours Dame," I whined as I felt an eruption coming on.

"I'm about to cum Dame!"

"Cum for daddy, baby." Dame said as he stroked my dick faster and faster.

Unable to hold it any longer, I came all over my sheets and Dame's hand. Dame used his nut covered hand to bring my face to his. He purposely put his hand inside of my mouth so I could taste myself, before he stuck his tongue down my throat, moaning at the taste.

Seconds later, Dame flipped me on my stomach, put one hand around my neck, and the other on my shoulder and fucked my soul out of my ass. I tried to keep my composure, because my sister was asleep in the other room and had no idea Dame was there.

Nobody knew about Dame and me, not even Sting. This was the first time I had ever kept a secret from her, but this is how Dame wanted it. Nobody knew of Dame's secret lifestyle, not even Caesar, and for the time being, this is how it had to be.

'Smack!'

Dame's hand went across my ass, and I instantly arched my back and threw it back on queue.

"That's it, baby! Throw that ass back for daddy," Dame said.

I loved when he talked nasty when we fucked. Nobody would ever believe a quiet, laid-back thug could be so vocal in the bedroom, or that he was gay for that matter.

"Like that daddy?" I said as I looked back at Dame and teased him with my extra-long tongue. Dame liked it when I exposed my wolf tongue when I sucked his dick or licked his ass. It turned him on immensely.

"Fucckkk!" he said as he neared an orgasm.

"You know that shit turn me on," Dame said as he pumped faster and harder inside of me. When he got excited, his dick gained several inches, and I could feel it in my stomach. I stroked my dick so I could cum with him again.

"I'm about to cum daddy, cum with me," I begged.

"I'm about to cum baby!" he advised.

I pushed off his dick and bent down and put his dick inside my mouth. Dame shook as he came and I swallowed all his nut, before I came again.

Dame pulled his dick out of my mouth and fell on the bed.

"Damn," was all he could say.

"I know right!" I said as I reached for the blunt and lighter on the nightstand.

I lit the blunt and took several pulls before passing it to Dame.

"Dame, what are we doing?"

"What do you mean?" he asked as he placed the blunt in his mouth and inhaled.

"How long do we have to keep our relationship a secret?"

"I can't answer that,"

"Well, I don't think I can continue to do this much longer," I stated.

"That's your choice," he responded as he inhaled the blunt again, grabbed my neck, and gave me a shotgun.

I inhaled the smoke and coughed up a lung.

"But I hope you give it careful consideration," Dame said before he tongued me down, and left me speechless.

I watched as he put on his clothes, looked out the bedroom door before he tiptoed out my room and out the front door.

"Damn, that nigga got some good ass dick?" I smiled as I jumped out the bed and sashayed around the room.

It felt good to be in my own spot. Well, technically, it was a spot I shared with my sister, Tonya. It wasn't that I didn't have love for Kris, but continuing to sleep on her mother's couch was a conflict of interest when it came to both of the crews. Kris and I made a deal to try to remain cool with each other, despite crew business. She didn't agree with what the guys had done to Sting, but she felt that she had nowhere to go. Blaze convinced her that the initiation was needed to prove her loyalty. When she called me crying, I figured she had finally grown tired of being under Blaze's dictatorship.

"Dash, I need you!" Kris cried.

"Girl, what's wrong?" I asked.

"It's Blaze. He beat me bad; can you come and get me? Nobody else answered their phones!" Kris whined.

"Why you ain't call the police, EMS, somebody else?" I asked suspiciously.

"Because I don't want him to go to jail, and I can't afford no damn extra bill. I just need help getting my things out of here, please!" Kris begged.

"Where are you at?"

"I'm at our new house on Drexel and Jefferson. I will send you the address," Kris responded.

"I'm on my way," I advised, before disconnecting the call.

My phone rang again, it was Sting.

"Hey boo!" I answered.

"Hey Dash, do you want to hit the mall with me?" Sting asked.

"I wish I could, but I have to rescue a damsel in distress, chile," I informed her.

"Who?"

"Kris. Blaze whooped her ass, and she needs me to help her get her things," I responded.

"What are you going to do, carry the shit on your back?" Sting laughed.

"Ha-ha, no. I'm going to use Tonya's car to get over there, then we're going to take her shit over to her mother's house," I informed her.

"I never knew Blake to beat women, but I guess it's not too farfetched if the motherfucker is out here raping bitches. Just be careful, in case it's a fucking trap," Sting warned.

"As a matter of fact, send me the address, in case I have to rescue your ass," Sting laughed.

"Okay I will text you the information," I laughed.

I love how overprotective Sting was, and I was just as overprotective when it came to her. I loved my sis, and there was nothing I wouldn't do for her.

"Love you, bro," Sting confessed.

"Love you, too." I responded and disconnected the call.

I knocked on Tonya's bedroom door. She responded in her sleepy voice.

"I need to use your car for an hour or so," I told her versus asking her.

"The keys are in my purse, on the table. I need my car back in three hours, tops. I got a few errands to run," Tonya stated.

"I will be back in two." I said as I grabbed her keys and headed out the door.

*****

I arrived at the worn-down house that looked like it had seen better days. There was no movement coming from inside. But there was a light coming from the bedroom. I turned off Tonya's car and headed up the porch. I knocked on the door and Kris opened it, not looking nowhere near as distraught as she sounded on the phone.

"Are you good?" I asked Kris.

"Yes, let me get my things," Kris responded and disappeared into a back room.

I looked around the dingy house. For the first time I noticed there was no furniture. Feeling uneasy, I decided to leave, but Slime and Blaze was on the other side of the door when I opened it.

"Going somewhere?" Blaze asked as he pushed me into the house.

"As a matter of fact, I am," I said and attempted to go around them.

"Nah, you ain't going anywhere, especially, after what you did to Thor," Blaze said.

"I don't know what you're talking about?" I informed him.

"That was your voice on Thor's Facebook live minutes before he was killed," Kris said as she walked up behind me.

"You scandalous bitch! You set me up?" I eyed Kris.

My eyes shifted and I felt the painful process of myself transitioning. Kris ran into the back room, and I ran after her. I was about to kill the backstabbing bitch, but Slime hit me in the back of the head. I charged him, knocking him to the ground. I fully transformed, opened my mouth, and started ripping his skin into shreds until he was no longer breathing.

A few minutes later, Blaze had transitioned as well, He picked me up and threw me across the room and slammed me against the wall. I regained my footing and stood up on my back legs. With Slime's blood leaking from my mouth, I walked towards Blaze.

"So, you're one of us? Did you think I was going to let you get away with what you did to Thor?" Blaze asked.

"What I did to Thor? Did you forget what you, Thor, and the rest of you dirty dick motherfuckers did to Sting?" I asked.

"It was part of the initiation process," Blaze stated.

"That's bullshit and you know it," I said as I tackled Blaze to the ground.

Blaze tossed me off him like I was a rag doll. He was much stronger than I was and had more experience as a werewolf than me.

Blaze charged and tore into my flesh. I grabbed his arm and tossed him off me. Blood was leaking from my chest when I stood up to face him.

"You looked like you're hurt pretty bad," Blaze taunted me.

"I will survive, you can't kill a bad bitch." I answered, trying to minimize the pain.

Blaze and I stared at each other down before we charged each other simultaneously.

I swung downward, connecting with Blaze's shoulder. He howled and fell to his knees. I bent down to go in for the kill and felt a sharp pain in my back and my chest. I looked down and saw the silver blade protruding from my chest. I turned around to see Kris standing there looking scared as fuck.

"You simple bitch!" I yelled as I fell to my knees.

"You broke the number one rule, loyalty," Kris said with a smirk on her face.

"Loyalty! You'd rather stay loyal to motherfucker that gang rapes women. You're a weak bitch! You and this grimy motherfucker deserve each other!" I yelled as I coughed up blood. My body was transitioning back into the human form.

"I'd rather be a weak bitch than a dead bitch!" Kris said as Blaze removed the

blade from my back and stabbed me in the heart.

I felt my life leave my body as I collapsed to the floor.

"I pray both you motherfuckers meet the same fate soon," I managed to say before I closed my eyes.

"We all will meet our makers one day, but not before your punk ass." Blaze added as he and Kris stepped over me and walked out the door leaving me to die next to Slime.

I thought about my mother, Tonya, Dame, Sting, and my father. I never got a chance to make amends with him.

I love you daddy. I'm sorry if I disappointed you. Please forgive me.

Chapter 13: Sting

I hadn't heard from Dash since he texted me his location earlier today, but that wasn't out of his norm. When he goes unheard of for long periods of time, it usually involves a man. But he didn't mention anything about seeing another man, just Kris.

Let me give him a call and make sure he's okay.

As I was getting ready to give Dash a call, my cell phone rang. It was his sister, Tonya.

"Hi Sting, have you heard from Dash today? He was only supposed to be gone for a couple of hours with my car, but that was five hours ago," Tonya said, sounding concerned.

"I haven't heard from him since earlier. He was supposed to meet up with Kris. Let me check his location," I replied as I checked the app.

"According to the app, Dash is still at the address he told me he was meeting Kris earlier today. I have a bad feeling about this," I confessed.

"So do I. Send me the address, I'm going to check it out," Tonya stated.

"Okay," I stated as I sent Tony the address and I advised her I would meet her there before disconnecting the call. I tried to call Dash phone, but it went to voicemail.

"What's going on?" Caesar asked. After Dash told me that he was not going to able to go to the mall with me I asked Caesar, and he was happy to come along.

"Dash said he was meeting with Kris hours ago. Dash told Tonya he would only be gone for two hours. I have a bad feeling about this," I said as my stomach turned into knots.

"Let's head over there, what's the address?" Caesar asked.

I rattled off the address and we were on our way.

*****

When we pulled onto the street, there were police everywhere. I jumped out before Caesar stopped the car and ran toward the house taped off with yellow tape. I ran towards Tonya. She was crying hysterically.

"Tonya, what's going on? I asked.

"He's dead, Sting!" Tonya yelled as she collapsed in my arms.

"What?" I said in disbelief.

"He can't be dead," I added.

"They said he's gone, and Slime, too!" Tonya cried.

"Slime is dead too?" I said, confused.

"Why did they have to kill him? He never did anything to anybody. He didn't deserve this," Tonya said as she cried.

I tried to console her, but reality sat in, and I started to cry as well. We both fell to the ground and consoled each other. There was a police lady processing information outside of the house. We made eye contact for a moment before she looked away hurriedly.

"What was going on?" Caesar asked.

"They're saying Dash is dead, Slime too," I cried.

The medical examiners came out of the house with two body bags on a gurney. Tonya screamed louder as the bodies were transported down the steps and placed in the back of the van.

"I need to see for myself!!" Tonya said as she broke free from me and tried to get to the bodies. Caesar had to restrain her.

"Let me go!" she screamed as she struggled to break free.

"Ma'am, please calm down. May I have your name?" the officer asked.

"My name is Tonya. I was told that my brother was dead! I need to know for sure!" Tonya cried harder.

"Do you have a picture of your brother?" she asked.

Tonya was shaking so bad; she couldn't get her phone out of her purse to give to the officer. I pulled out my phone, went to my gallery, and showed the officer a picture of Dash and me.

"This is him," I said as I held my phone out for her to see.

I silently prayed she didn't confirm one of those bodies was my best friend.

The officer looked at the picture, then looked at Tonya and me.

"I'm sorry to inform you that your brother is one of the deceased we found inside the home," the officer advised.

"Noooooo!" Tonya cried.

"Dash!" I cried as I rushed to the van.

"Please God, no!"

"I got you baby. We're going to get to the bottom of this, I promise," Caesar said as held me in his chest.

I felt so bad for Tonya. I didn't know how she was going to break the news to her mother and her father.

"I'm so sorry for your loss. Do you know of anyone that would want to hurt your brother?" she asked.

"No, everybody loved Dash," Tonya sobbed.

"What is your brother's full name?" the officer asked.

"Dillan Chavers Jr. Is Slime dead too?"

"Excuse me, Slime?" The officer looked confused.

"Someone said Slime was the other body found inside the house," Tonya said as she fumbled through her Facebook page and showed the detective a picture of Slime.

"Unfortunately, he is the other deceased person found inside the home, but I can't confirm if he was the killer or another victim. We have reason to believe there was at least one more person inside the home when the murders took place. I'm sorry, that's all the information I can give out at this time, but here is my card. Give me a call if you can think of anything else that can be helpful, my name is Lieutenant Jordan Masters," she said as she handed Tonya her card.

Tonya placed it inside of her purse as the lieutenant walked away.

"How am I going to tell my parents Dash is dead?" Tonya cried.

"We can do it together," I informed her as I grabbed her hands.

"Thank you." Tonya said.

Caesar rubbed my shoulders and kissed me softly on the neck. I turned around and looked into his beautiful eyes. I was about to tell him I was going to ride with Tonya, but he read my mind.

"How about you ride with Tonya to her parent's house? I will meet y'all there," Caesar said softly.

"Thank you, babe." I kissed him on his lips.

He kissed me back, gave Tonya his condolences, and walked to the car. Tonya and I walked to her car, hand, and hand.

*****

Dash's parents took the news hard, but his father took it the hardest because they never had the opportunity to repair their relationship. I sat with the family for as long as I could, but the crying was too much for me to handle. I snuck out of the house while they were consoling one another.

Caesar was sitting on the hood of the car waiting for me. I ran into his arms and broke down crying.

"This is so unfair. How am I supposed to live without my friend," I cried.

"Like he would want you to live life to the fullest," Caesar said.

"I'm going to kill that bitch. She set him up, I know she did," I advised Caesar.

"Cut off the head and the body will die. Without Blaze, the rest of the crew is nothing. With Thor and Slime gone, we only have three more to get rid of," Caesar said.

"Four! Kris got to fucking go, too. There's no way she will continue to walk this earth when my best friend is dead!" I yelled.

"Okay but promise me that you won't do anything until WE come up with a plan. I just found you, I wouldn't be able to live with myself if something happened to you," Caesar informed me as he looked into my eyes.

"I promise baby. I love you," I smiled before Caesar pulled me into his chest.

"I love you too, Sierra."

Caesar opened the passenger side door for me, before he climbed in the driver's side seat, and pulled off.

I stared out the window and tried to come up with the most brutal and gruesome way to kill Blaze and Kris. Caesar was correct, I knew Dash wanted me to live my life to the fullest. After I made sure everybody involved paid for what they had done to him.

*****

Dash's funeral was packed. He was dressed in a purple suit, with a red, black, and green sash draped over his left shoulder, representing the Howling Huskies. His face was beat to the Gods, just like he liked it. Dash's father preached the eulogy until he broke down crying. Mrs. Chaver's consoled her husband as the assisting pastor stepped up to the podium and completed the sermon.

None of the Seven Mile Wolf Pack was dumb enough to show their faces at the funeral despite the friendship a few of them maintained with Dash. If they had shown up, there would have been nobody that could stop me from murdering them inside of Dash's father's church.

I watched Dame out of my peripheral view. Outside of me, he was the only Howling Husky that shed a tear for Dash.

Why was Dame so emotional over Dash's death? The only interaction I ever witnessed between them was "hi" and "bye".

Caesar and I were so in sync that he picked up on what I was putting down by following my eyes and paying attention to my facial expressions.

"I ain't never saw that nigga cry before. What's up with that shit?" Caesar whispered.

"Shhh! Don't be cussing in church, but I was thinking the same thing," I said.

I can tell Caesar wanted to get down to the bottom of it. I placed my hand on his knee and shook my head for him to let it go. He relaxed and pulled me closer.

Mr. Chavers allowed the Howling Huskies to be the pallbearers. I led them out of the church, and to the horse and carriage that was carrying Dash to his final resting place. One of the ladies that attended started singing Yolanda Adam's "His Eye is on the Sparrow" as the crew placed Dash's body inside the glass carriage. When she hit the high note, half of the congregation lost it, and broke down. Mr.'s Chaver's had to be carried away from the carriage by a team of choir members. I cried in Caesar's arms before he led me to the car so we could ride closely behind the horse and carriage.

When the carriage started to move, I think my heart stopped beating. Not for the loss of life, or from the pain I was feeling inside, but from the pain I was going to inflict on certain members of the Seven Mile Wolf Pack. There was no turning back now.

*****

I sat outside of Kris's mother's house and waited for Kris's mother to leave to go play Keno with her girlfriends. Dash told me on the days Kris mother left for long periods of time, Kris snuck Kold in so they could fuck. He also told me that Kris's mother also kept a key to the house under the doormat on the porch.

Like clockwork, Kold knocked, and Kris opened the door wearing a tank top and some boy shorts. They kissed each other before going inside and closing the door behind them. I gripped my knife in my hand and rubbed the letters engraved on the blade of the knife with my gloved hands.

I walked around the house to see if I could see what Kris and Kold were doing. I wasn't sure if either of them was werewolves, but I was prepared in case they were. When I looked inside of the bedroom window, Kris was on her knees giving Kold a blowjob. I watched them through the window for a few minutes. From the look of his mediocre dick, I could tell he wasn't part werewolf. I crept back to the front porch and grabbed the key under the mat and placed it inside the keyhole. Once I was inside, I followed the sounds of ass smacking and moaning. The house was dark except for a few candles Kris lit to set the mood.

Kold had Kris bent over the bed as he fucked her doggy-style. Kris moaned and talked shit as Kold fucked her long and hard. My nails extended from my skin and were sharp as knives. He was in pure ecstasy as he held on to her hips and fucked her with his eyes close. I lifted my arm above my head, came down fast, and sliced Kold's dick off. He screamed, then passed out when he saw all the blood squirting from what was left of his dick. The other part of his dick was still hanging out of Kris's pussy. She turned around and saw Kold lying on the ground. She screamed when she saw the blood leaking from the hole where Kold's dick used to be. Kris noticed Kold's dick hanging out of her pussy and snatched it out. She screamed at the sight of the bloody dick in her hand. I ripped the dick out of her hand and shoved it in her mouth. Kold started to move so I bent down, ripped his heart out of his chest and made Kris watch as it exploded as I squeezed it in my hand. She backed away as I walked toward her.

"How could you do that to Dash? Why would you set him up? He loved you," I asked as I walked towards her.

Kris mumbled something, but I couldn't understand what she was saying with a mouth full of dick. I slapped her hard across her face, causing the dick to fly across the room. She needed to explain why she lured Dash to his death before I sent her to meet her maker.

"Why?" I asked her again.

"Blaze made me do it. He said he was going to kill me," Kris confessed.

"You lured him to his death. You could've called it off at any time, but you didn't," I cried.

"He killed Thor! What the fuck did you think was going to happen? If we didn't retaliate, we would look like some pussies," Kris yelled as blood and spit flew from her mouth.

"He killed him for me! Because of what Blaze and the rest of the crew did to me!" I screamed.

"Is that right? Well, I guess that means his blood is on your hands, not mine," Kris said with hate in her eyes.

"Whose hands is your blood on?" I asked.

"What?" She said, confused.

I charged Kris and used all my mutant strength to beat the fuck out of her. She tried to fight back, but she was no match for me. Blood painted the walls with each blow that landed upon Kris's body. She whimpered as she lay on the ground.

"Fuck you. Blaze is going to kill your ass, just like he killed Dash," Kris said as spit up blood.

"Guess what bitch, you won't be around to see it," I said as I removed my silver blade and stabbed Kris in the heart. Her mouth opened as she reached for the knife and tried to remove it, but she didn't have enough strength to do so. Her arms fell to her side, and she died looking at the person that made it happen.

"Tell Dash I said hi, bitch," I said as I walked out of the room and left the house.

Chapter 14: Sasha

When I saw her at the crime scene, my heart stopped. I was face to face with my baby girl whom I abandoned so many years ago. Although I hadn't seen her, physically, since she was three years old, I knew it was her. I lost track of her when Stephen moved out of the apartment we once shared together. I relied on my connections, investigators, and Facebook to keep updated on my daughter's life. I thought about the day I walked out of her and Stephen's life.

I crept inside the apartment around five o'clock in the morning, like I did on many mornings, after sleeping around with different men. Usually, I could lie my way out of it, but Stephen wasn't going for it this time. He pressed me about where I had been and who I was with. And when I came up with some bullshit lie, he wanted me to prove that it was true. I grew tired of lying and finally told him the truth. Stephen gave me an ultimatum, stay home, and raise our daughter, or leave. I chose the streets, and I never

looked back. I never got a chance to kiss Sierra goodbye.

Seeing Sierra at the crime scene brought out so many emotions. When Jordan asked me to interview Dillan Chaver's sister, I had no problem doing so, until I saw Sierra.

"You know what, Jordan. I think you should take this one," I advised her.

"Why?" she asked.

"I know the family of the deceased. I don't want to compromise the case. Especially if we're dealing with a serial killer." I informed her.

Jordan didn't think anything about it and interviewed the sister of the victim as Sierra and her guy friend stood nearby. I stayed in the background and waited for Jordan to complete her interview and the trio to leave before I approached Jordan.

"Do they have any helpful information we can use?" I asked.

"No. Just the basic shit. Everybody loved him, he was a good man, and wouldn't hurt a fly, type shit," Jordan answered.

"What about the other girl and her boyfriend? Who are they to the victim?" I asked.

"She was the best friend of Dillan Chavers," Jordan added.

"Okay," I simply replied.

"Which one of them do you know?" Jordan asked.

"I went to school with his sister," I lied.

"Oh okay. Maybe you should go talk to the parents tomorrow. They may feel more comfortable talking to you out of familiarity," Jordan suggested.

"I will think about it. First, I need to get back to the office. These cases got to be related to each other." I said as I headed to my car before Jordan could object. I felt like we were close to breaking the case and needed to buckle down. More importantly, I needed to find out if Sierra was involved in the case and how.

I hated coming into the office during normal business hours because it was always hectic. Upset family members lined the lobby, missing person reports being filed, and unruly young adults booked for disorderly conduct riddled the precinct every day. I kept my head down as I made my way to my office in the back of the precinct tucked in a small corner away from everybody else. I closed and locked the door behind me, then shut the blinds so I could be free from distractions.

Then I grabbed the box labeled "Mangled Murders", placed it on my desk, and removed the contents. I put the bags of evidence on one side of the table and the reports on the other side, before I opened my computer and clicked the icon to open my emails. I was expecting the phone records from Dash's and Thor's phone. I put on a pair of gloves as I grabbed the first bag of evidence from the Theodore "Thor" Johnson murder.

I flipped through the phone and saw lots of pictures of their crew as well as shit I didn't want to see like nude pictures, orgies, and drug use. I shook my head as I thumbed through the phone until I heard a young lady crying. There was a group of men gathered around her. Thor recorded as the other men gagged her and took turns raping her. I zoomed in to get a better look of the girl.

Oh my God! Sierra!

I gasped and dropped the phone on my desk. I couldn't take seeing my baby girl hurt so badly. I picked the phone up and came across a Facebook Live video. The Facebook video shows him talking shit before being struck from behind. The phone flew from his hand, and I heard Thor being taunted by his killer. I didn't recognize the voice, but the killer made it clear he was going to kill him for raping his friend. Moments later, I heard screaming, silence, and then the voice of an older woman trying to find out what was going on. The last thing I saw was a glimpse of a furry animal of some sort with a long snout, who stepped on the phone as he walked away.

I put the phone down and pulled at the contents of the other evidence bag. It contained fur and a long toenail.

Do werewolves really exist?

I flopped down in my chair and thought about all the evidence that was recovered and how it connected. Then I thought about my baby girl that I had abandoned and the traumatic shit she's endured as a result. I cried, and asked for her forgiveness, because I would never be able to forgive myself if she didn't.

*****

A hard knock at the door woke me out of my sleep. I jumped up, unaware of my surroundings. I looked at the time and saw that it was past midnight. I stood up, stretched, and opened the door. It was one of the guys from the midnight shift. He was young and very nice looking. Any other time I would have made a pass at him, but I was too drained, and Sierra's well-being was weighing heavy on my mind.

"Detective Grant, Lieutenant Masters thought I would find you here. She wanted me to inform you that there have been two more murders, with the same motives as the others. She wants you over at the scene as soon as possible, here's the address," The cutie said as he handed me a piece of paper.

"Thank you." I said as I looked at the address.

This is the same neighborhood Sierra lives in. What the hell is going on?

I grabbed my phone and purse and headed out the door.

Twenty-five minutes later, I pulled up to the scene. The crowd started to form and a person I assumed was the mother of one of the victims was crying hysterically in the arms of a loved one. I showed the waiting officer my badge, ducked under the tape, and proceeded inside the home.

Jordan was talking to one of the officers on the scene. I tried to walk past her, but she excused herself from the officer and grabbed my arm. I looked down at my arm then back at Jordan, and she let go of me.

"I stopped by last night, you weren't home," Jordan stated as if I owed her an explanation.

"What's your point?" I asked her.

"I wanted to talk to you about something," Jordan lied as she licked her lips.

"Obviously, I wasn't there," I said as I attempted to walk past her.

I stopped in my tracks and turned around to address her.

"And the next time you have something you want to talk to me about, call first, don't just show up at my house again. Those days are over with," I said as I walked off.

"Sasha! Sasha!" Jordan called out, but I ignored her and continued to talk through the house in search of the murder scene.

The first thing I saw when I entered the bedroom was blood splattered all over the bedroom. I grabbed a pair of gloves out of my back pocket and surveyed the bedroom as I put them on. There were two dead victims, on opposite sides of the room. The man was bleeding from his groin area, where his dick used to be. His heart was ripped out of his chest and his eyes and mouth were wide open, as if he was surprised by his killer. The lady was beaten, sliced, and stabbed to death. I could tell by the amount of damage done to her body that killing her was personal.

A glimpse of something shined in my peripheral as I looked across the room. It was part of the knife that wasn't covered in blood. I walked over to the body and bent down.

It can't be! How the hell did it get here?

I took a hard look at the badly beaten face of the woman that stared back at me with lifeless eyes, and my heart skipped a beat. I walked over to the other body and looked at the young man looking back at me, and gasped. I recognized both people from Thor's Facebook page. They were both members of the Seven Mile Wolf Pack.

Who wanted all members of the crew dead, and why?

Baffled for a minute, I decided to walk outside and get some air. When I turned to walk out the room, another glimpse of the piece of metal shined in my eye again, stopping me in my tracks.

"No, it couldn't be! Please, God no!" I whispered as I turned and looked back at the deceased woman again.

Chapter 15: Sting

I laid in Caesar's arms and watched the eleven o'clock news. The words "breaking news" flashed across the screen, followed by the news anchor.

"Two bodies were discovered in the bedroom of a home in the home of Berkshire and Mack. Police say the victims, Kodell Roberts, and Kristina Willard, were in their early twenties. Currently there are no suspects." said the news anchor.

I noticed the same two lady officers in the background were the same two ladies at Slime's and Dash murder scene as well.

Do they think they're fucking with a serial killer or something?

Caesar must read my mind.

"Do you think the police are stupid enough to believe that all these murders are done by one person?" he asked.

182

"I don't know, but it seems that way, and that can be good or bad," I responded.

"Why is that?"

"Because if they try to put all the murders on one person, they can go away for a long fucking time," I said in a somber tone.

"Hopefully, they were careful and didn't put themselves in a position to get caught up," Caesar said as he stared at me.

I hated he knew me so well in such a short period of time.

"Sierra, what did you do?" Caesar questioned.

"I might have fucked up," I confessed.

"What do you mean 'you may have fucked up', Sierra?" Caesar scolded me.

"I left the knife my father gave me in Kris's chest," I spat out.

"You did what! Why would you do that?" Caesar yelled.

"I blanked out! After I beat the fuck out of her, the bitch was still talking shit, so I stabbed her ass!" I confessed.

"Okay, your fingerprints aren't in the system because you've never been arrested. There are plenty of knives out there. They can't link it to you," Caesar said, relieved.

"It was engraved with me and my dad's initials," I said ashamed.

"Sierra, what the fuck!" Caesar said as he jumped out the bed.

"Caesar, calm down, please! You're making me nervous. I know I fucked up!" I cried.

I watched Caesar as he paced the floor. I had never seen him so stressed, not even when we spoke about the plan to take down Blaze.

"Fuck it, there's nothing we can do about it now. If anybody asks, tell them you lost it a few months back," Caesar instructed as he sat next to me.

He still looked worried enough for both of us. I didn't give a fuck if I went to jail for killing Kris, if I was able to kill Blaze ass as well. What I did care about was leaving Caesar alone because we were inseparable since we met, and I was in love with him.

I removed my clothes and straddled Caesar. His face and body language told me he wasn't in the mood, but his dick had a mind of its own.

"I'm sorry I was so careless, baby," I whined as I kissed his face and neck.

"I can't lose you, Sierra," he answered in a low tone.

"You won't baby, I promise," I assured him.

I scooted off Caesar's lap and onto the floor in front of him and removed his dick from his joggers.

"Sierra, not now," he asserted as he tried to push me away.

I ignored him, put his dick inside my mouth, and went to work. Caesar stopped resisting and allowed me to please him.

"Damn, baby," he said as he grabbed the back of my head and pushed me further in his lap.

I gagged, repeatedly as his dick hit the back of my tonsils. I hated it when Caesar was mad at me, so if using my tonsils as a punching bag is what he needed to do to relieve some frustration, I was going to take that beating like Gervonta Davis.

Caesar pulled his dick out of my mouth and stood up over me.

"Get up," he said as his eyes shifted, and removed his clothes.

He grabbed me by my arm and flung me to the bed, face first. The amount of force he used let me know that he was very upset and was about to take it out on my pussy. There was nothing more for me to do than to brace myself for the punishment I was about to receive for being careless and hotheaded.

Without warning, Caesar transitioned into a werewolf and let out an angry howl. Because I had never seen that side of him, I tried to run away, but he grabbed my foot, jumped on my back, and shoved his massive hybrid dick inside of me. I screamed as his dick bombarded my pussy walls and poked the top of my navel. Drool dripped on my back as he fucked the shit out of me, hard and long. He reached his hairy arms around my neck and blew his hot breath onto my neck.

"Punish me daddy, punish this pussy for being a bad girl," I begged.

I could feel Caesar's dick grow several more inches inside of me, to the point it would be unbearable to an average woman. When Caesar stuck his nails in my

shoulders, I howled from the pain, and transitioned as well.

Caesar fucked me so hard, I almost passed out

during my transition. He unexpectedly pulled his dick out

of me, and it caused me to look back at him to see what

was wrong. The fire in his eyes said it all. He was furious

with me.

"Bend the fuck over," he growled.

I dug into the mattress with my nails, turned away,

and anticipated what was about to happen next.

Caesar forced his dick inside of my ass causing me

to let out a piercing howl as he growled and pounded my

insides. Once the pain subsided, I matched his energy by

bucking towards him.

"Harder!" I growled.

Caesar thrusted harder against me, knocking me off

balance. He jumped on top of my back and long dicked me

for twenty minutes straight. I could feel a puddle forming

under me as I pissed myself and came repeatedly. I had

never felt something that hurt so good in my life. It made

me wonder why we hadn't fucked in our werewolf state

sooner. The adrenaline alone made me cum harder than

I've ever had.

In a quick motion, Caesar flipped me over and sat

me on top of his dick.

"Fuck me until I tell you to stop," he commanded.

I followed his wishes and bounced up and down on

his dick as he held my hips tight. His dick was so big, that I

chose to only go halfway down, but he wasn't having it.

Each time I tried to go halfway down; Caesar pushed me

further down until I reached the shaft of his dick.

"That's it, now rock on this dick, back and forth,"

he said as he helped me with my efforts.

The friction of his dick rubbing against my clit,

made me come back-to-back. Before I realized it, I had lost

control and was back bouncing on his dick. Caesar tried to

regain control, but there was nothing he could do. I was in full werewolf mode, and I had the strength of a hundred men.

"Tell me you forgive me," I demanded.

Caesar growled but didn't say anything. I tightened the walls of my pussy and bounced more aggressively.

"Baby, please tell me you forgive me," I pleaded as I licked his face and massaged his balls.

"Shit! I forgive you," he managed to say.

"Say it louder!"

"I forgive you, Sierra!" he screamed as he gripped my thighs, pumped harder and came inside of me.

I bounced harder as I prepared to cum as well.

"I'm about to cum, Cease," I squirmed before I came all over Caesar.

Caesar grabbed me around my waist and rested his head on my back.

"I love you Sierra, we can't fuck up again. This shit with Blaze must go as planned. If something happens to you, I don't know how I would be able to live with myself," Caesar mumbled.

"You don't have to worry about that, because I swear, I will never leave you. Everything will be fine, I promise." I reassured Caesar.

I curled up in Caesar's arms as he laid on the pillow. I rubbed his head as he snored. His ability to let his problems fall by the waist side and go to sleep amazed me, because my mind raced as I replayed Blaze's murder in my head over again.

A smile and a sense of calmness overtook me as I envisioned Blaze dying, and I was going to the one who killed him.

*****

We waited until darkness came before we headed to the woods. Tonight, there was going to be a full moon, so there was no time like the present to take Blaze out and close this chapter of my life. Caesar talked Blaze into meeting him in the woods, alone, so they could talk things over and consider a possible truth between packs. I made Caesar promise me that Blaze would be my kill, and he agreed.

Caesar's plan was to get to the woods before Blaze to make sure there weren't any surprises waiting on him. What we didn't expect was for Blaze to be there waiting. Thankfully I followed Caesar's instructions and waited five minutes before I followed him in the woods. I waited at a distance when I heard Blaze's voice.

"I thought you might try to get here early, so I beat you to the punch. What is it that you want to talk about?" Blaze asked.

"I think it's time to call it truth, before anybody else gets hurt," Caesar responded.

"It's a little too late for this don't you think? Y'all killed off my entire pack, and now you want to call truths? Fuck that, we will call it truth's when our numbers are even in death. Let's see, we already took out that faggot ass nigga, Dash. After I take out that nigga, Dame, I'm going to kill your bitch, after I get some more of that good pussy." Blaze said as he smirked.

It took everything in my human being to remain calm when Blaze used my trauma to get under Caesar's skin. I couldn't believe he would stoop so low and degrade me worse than he already did.

"That won't ever happen again, and if you ever bring up MY woman again, I will rip that smirk off your face just like we did your boy," Caesar warned Blaze.

"Fuck your truths," Blaze challenged as he walked toward Caesar.

"I thought you would say that." Caesar smiled.

That was my cue to appear from behind the tree, I had been waiting behind. When I appeared by Caesar's side, Blaze let out a hearty laugh.

"You brought your bitch to fight your battles?" Blaze laughed.

"No, he brought his bitch to fight another bitch," I responded. The clouds were dispersing. In a few minutes, the moon would be at its peak. I removed my clothes and exposed my naked body. I had ruined too many fly outfits, by not stripping before I transitioned.

"Damn girl, you got body for days. I mean I only saw the back of your ass when I was fucking the shit out of you," Blazed laughed.

Before Blaze could close his mouth, Caesar caught him off guard and hit him in his mouth. Blaze stumbled and spat out a mouth of blood before he charged Caesar. I watched as Blaze and Caesar rolled around in the dirt. The stars danced in the sky as the moon illuminated the woods and everything around it. My skin burned as my bones bulged and my nails cut through my skin.

Blaze jumped on top of Caesar and strangled him. I charged Blaze, knocking him on his back. He stood on his back legs and transitioned into a werewolf. Caesar matched his energy and transitioned as well. We all stared at each other before Caesar, and I jumped Blaze and put the paws on him. During the entanglement Blaze broke free. He had several slashes across his chest and was bleeding badly.

"It takes the both of you to jump me. The Huskies are a bunch of pussies." Blaze taunted.

Caesar and I looked at each other, and I gave him the go ahead to pounce. I wasn't no dummy, I was a woman and Blaze was still a man, werewolf or not he was stronger than I was. Caesar's job was to tender and tire Blaze out, so I could go in for the kill, literally.

Caesar and Blaze were scratching, biting, and punching one another. Everything was going in Caesar's favor until Blaze scooped up a pile of dirt and threw it into Caesar's eyes, temporarily blinding him. Blaze took advantage and latched onto Caesar's neck and started shaking him like a rag doll. Caesar looked helpless as Blaze sank his teeth in his flesh.

I picked up a fallen limb and struck Blaze hard across the back. He didn't let go off Caesar, so I struck him until he released Caesar from his grip. Caesar lay on the ground, motionless. I crawled to his side and called out his name, but he didn't respond.

I felt a sharp pain across my back and the burning sensation of my flesh ripping open. I stood and faced my enemy.

"It's just you and me, bitch," Blaze said as he licked his chops and freed his mouth of Caesar's blood.

I charged Blaze like a bull and rammed my head into his chest, then butted his chin with my head, causing him to stumble into the wall. Not giving him a chance to react, I reigned blow after blow onto Blaze's body. He managed to block one of my blows and hit me with an uppercut that sent me flying into a tree. I hit my head and slid to the ground. Out of my blurry eyes, I saw Blaze coming toward me, but I couldn't move.

Blaze picked me up and threw me back to the other side of the woods. As he walked toward me, Caesar grabbed his leg. Blaze kicked the shit out of Caesar's face, knocking him out. His stall allowed me time to regain strength and ready myself for Blaze's attack. I stood up and growled loudly, Blaze did the same. We both charged each other at the same time and locked our canine teeth into each other's flesh. I felt a piece of flesh being ripped from my body and screamed out in pain, as a piece of Blaze's flesh fell from my mouth.

I stumbled backwards and Blaze roundhouse the shit out of me. I spun around twice before I hit the ground. Blaze wrapped his massive paws around my neck. I struggled to breathe as he choked the hell out of me. I saw a woman standing over me but couldn't make out who it was because my vision was blurry. She held something large inside of her hands. Seconds later, it came down, crashing on the top of Blaze's head. She repeated the process until Blaze was no longer moving. I looked in awe at the woman that had just finished bashing Blaze's head. I didn't know if I was happy that she saved my life or pissed that she potentially took my kill.

"Who are you? Why are you here?" I asked.

"My name is Sasha. I'm here to help you,"

"Why?"

"Sierra, can we grab your friend and talk about this later? Before he wakes up," Sasha answered, looking down at Blaze. I looked at Caesar and saw he was moving.

Thank God.

"How do you know my name? Wait a minute, I remember you. You are one of the cops at Dash's crime scene. How do you know me?" I asked as I advanced towards her in a threatened manner.

"You are my daughter, Sierra," Sasha said as she backed away.

"Liar!" I said as I pounced on her and growled.

"Sierra, I promise. I'm your mother. I abandoned you when you were only three years old. I'm sorry!"

"So why the hell are you back? Nobody wants you here," I asked, sobbing as I hovered over her body.

"An opportunity presented itself in the Detroit Police Department, and I took it. I never meant to disrupt your life,"

"Disrupt my life?" I laughed.

"You could never disrupt my life. I could never miss what I don't remember having."

"You're right, Sierra. I totally understand," Sasha agreed.

"Sierra!" Caesar called out weakly.

I ran to his side and hugged him.

"Thank God you are all right, Caesar," I yelled.

I didn't see Blaze jump up, but Caesar did.

"Sierra look out," he said above a whisper.

I turned and saw Blaze charging toward me.

"Sierra!" Sasha called out.

I turned and saw her holding the same knife I used to kill Kris. She threw it at me at full force. I caught the knife in the air, seconds before Blaze reached me.

I stabbed Blaze in the mouth. I was still holding onto the knife as Blaze struggled to get free. I worked the knife back and forth as I wrestled to free it from Blaze's mouth. When I was finally able to free the knife from his mouth, I stuck the knife deep inside of his heart, and twisted. I pushed him back to the tree and drove the knife deeper into his skin. Blaze stopped struggling, his arms fell to his side, and he took his last breath.

When I removed the knife, Blaze's limp body fell to the ground and transitioned back into human form. I walked over to Caesar and helped him to his feet. He leaned on me as we began to walk out of the woods.

"Sierra, I can't let you leave like this. I have to turn you in," Sasha yelled after me.

I propped Caesar against a nearby tree. He transitioned back into human form as I walked toward Sasha, transitioning with each step.

"You can, and you will, and you want to know why? One, you owe me. Two, this knife should have been stored in evidence and not in your possession. Three, if you don't let me go, I will kill your ass, mother or not. So, what's it going to be, mother?" I warned her.

Sasha remained silent and looked away.

"That's what I thought," I smirked as I turned away and went to help Caesar.

I wrapped my arms around him and limped out of the forest leaving Sierra alone with Blaze's body.

When I walked away from Sasha, I felt nothing. No bond, no heartbreak, or no connection. I had no love to give to the woman that abandoned me or my father. The only thing I had to give was a cold shoulder and a colder heart.

Prologue: Sierra

Caesar and I are still the King and Queen of The Howling Huskies and are awaiting the arrival of our little Prince. Caesar Dash Jacobs will be making his debut in this world in four months, and I couldn't be happier. Feeling my son move inside of my belly warmed my heart and created an unbreakable bond. I could never do to my son what my mother had done to me.

Me and my mother's relationship was still a work in progress. She started counseling and insisted on being there every step of the way for her grandchild. At first, I didn't want her anywhere in my life or my baby's life, but my daddy and Caesar convinced me to at least give it a try, and I'm glad that I did, because I've learned that I am more like her than I thought.

Sasha was able to close all the cases and link them to the Seven Mile Wolf Pack because they no longer existed. Based on the evidence Sasha and her crew collected, we could've easily been locked up under the jail, so I am forever thankful.

Today was my birthday and my entire family came together to celebrate. We sat around daddy's house and ate, drank, played cards, and sang karaoke. Sasha and my daddy got along well, probably a little too well. When they were slowly dancing, I could have sworn I saw them stare in each other's eyes. When I was about to interrupt, Caesar grabbed me by my arm, and pulled me close.

"Where do you think you're going?" Caesar asked, smiling.

"Do you see how close my daddy and Sasha are getting? Ugghhh! I can't let them do this," I responded as I tried to pull away from Caesar.

"You can and you will. The only person you need to worry about is our little prince inside of you and your husband," Caesar said.

"Husband? Boy, stop playing," I laughed.

Caesar got down on one knee and pulled a ring box out of his pocket.

"I love you Sierra. You are the mother of my child, and you will forever have my heart. Will you marry me?" Caesar asked as he opened the box and presented a beautiful engagement ring.

I screamed and jumped up and down, getting everybody's attention.

"Girl, my knees are starting to buckle. Will you be my wife or not?" Caesar laughed.

"Yes, of course I will marry you," I yelled as I jumped into his arms and kissed him deeply.

Afterwards, we stared into each other's eyes. Caesar eyes shifted, and so did mine.

"I look forward to raising our little wolf together," I said.

"Me too, and I look forward to spending forever with you." Caesar said as he kissed and hugged me.

Sasha and daddy joined Caesar and I in our hug as we said hello to new beginnings and goodbye to old memories as we celebrated the expansion of our family and to making the Howling Huskies stronger than ever.

Also, by the Author:

Dilemmas: If Loving You is Wrong (Part 1)

Amazon.com: Dilemmas: If Loving You Is Wrong eBook: Kinn-Tarver, Crystal: Kindle Store

Dilemmas: Courtney's Revenge (Part 2)

Amazon.com: Dilemmas: Courtney's Revenge eBook: Kinn-Tarver, Crystal: Kindle Store

The Dom: Her Game, Your Rules

Amazon.com: The Dom : Her Game, Your Rules ... eBook : Kinn-Tarver, Crystal: Kindle Store

Baby Mama Chronicles: Rider's Story

Baby Mama Chronicles: Rider's Story - Kindle edition by Tarver, C.K.. Literature & Fiction Kindle eBooks @ Amazon.com.

A Psycho Love

Amazon.com: A Psycho Love eBook : Tarver, C.K.: Kindle Store

Made in the USA
Middletown, DE
28 October 2023

41401258R00116